Àshàké

A Riveting Tale Of Redemptive Love

STANLEY ORJI

Printed in the Federal Republic of Nigeria

First Printing, 2022

ISBN 979-836-705-425-5

Cradle Creed Books

Author's Website: stanleyorji.com

"This book is a work of fiction and the characters are imaginary. Although certain establishments, public institutions and agencies have been mentioned, along with some of their officers, the actual characters are the author's creation. As such, any resemblance to individuals, living or dead, is purely coincidental. Actions and opinions are also understood to be those of the characters."

Cover Art: Miriam Sunday

Cover Design: oladelegraphics.com

ACKNOWLEDGMENT

For all the fights she 'invested' to make this book happen, for her invaluable inputs both for the cover design and the content of this book, and, above all, for being such a loyal friend over the years; a big THANK YOU to the super-smart Eme 'Handmaid' Ezeliora.

There will be many more…

DEDICATION

In loving memory of Austin Ndubuisi Orji; an eagle shot down in flight.

We have forgiven, but we will always remember.

SECTION

Bliss

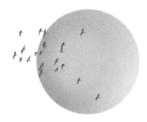

CHAPTER 1

Àshàké woke up slowly.

Her mind, out of habit, swung into 'day planner' mode: switch on the heater, pray, take out the trash... But something was different; everything was.

The chill of the air-conditioner, the sheer softness of the satin bed sheets, and the weight of the duvet on her naked body. The light was dim but through the slightly parted cream curtains of *Chalet 5*, the fronds of the giant king palm just outside the window produced a shifting kaleidoscope of light shafts on the back of the settee.

She could tell it was morning.

The bathroom door was ajar and above the sound of running water, she could hear Kamsy singing *Mercy Said No* in his booming voice. It was the morning after. She and Kamsy were on their honeymoon. She was officially Mrs. Àshàké Kamsiyochi-Ezeani.

It actually happened.

Last night after they arrived at the Chalet and Kamsy took her in his arms and pressed his lips to hers, she had thought for a fleeting moment that she was going to wake up and everything would dissolve into nothingness as was typical of many of her dreams in childhood where she would awake just as she was about to obtain her quest; but not this time.

She knew she wasn't going to wake up. She didn't want to. Ever!

She had expected Kamsy's tenderness but not his dexterity as he gently caressed the skin of her bare arms and then kneaded the tense muscles between her shoulder blades through the thin lace of the bridal dress; all the while holding her against his stirring maleness in a gentle firm embrace. The kiss was their first, yet it was not tentative. His touch was deliberate; his movement unhurried.

When the wedding dress eventually dropped around her ankles in a heap of concentric folds and Kamsy lifted her with an easy sweeping motion to carry her to the bed, multiple bursts of sweetness exploded on her inside.

Àshàké had looked forward to the 'you may kiss the bride' ritual at the solemnization but it was not to be. Pastor Jaye, the resident pastor at Sanctification Chapel, was brusque and business-like. "Read those aloud," he said as he handed each of them the well-worn identical laminated A4-sized sheets that contained the vows. Pointing to Kamsy, he said, "You first." It was surreal. They weren't even told to face each other.

Later, as they stepped down from the altar to be photographed with the clergymen and their spouses, she whispered to Kamsy under her breath, "That felt like swearing an oath in court." "The end justifies the means," he said with a sly grin.

She opened her eyes and took in her surroundings in the dim light as she self-consciously pulled up the duvet to cover her shoulders. Her wedding dress was draped carelessly on the arm of the couch, the long shafts of light from the slightly open curtains now forming a pattern on it. The rest of her clothes were still strewn on the floor as if some film director had arranged them for romantic effect. Kamsy's clothes lay in an untidy heap at the foot of the bed. He appeared to have made a half-hearted attempt at orderliness.

Her body felt drained but there was an unfamiliar glow on her inside that made her want to laugh out loud.

CHAPTER 2

The wedding reception was both boring and exhausting but she had tried hard to smile through it.

Although she hadn't looked forward to the ceremonies, she had braced herself for the inevitable accompaniments of a high society wedding in the Nigerian south. Her ordeal began with the photo session. First, with seemingly unending groups of unfamiliar relatives - most of them from Kamsy's massive extended family.

Those who posed as members of her own family were mostly her mother's customers and friends from her Ajagun neighborhood. There were a few younger people she only vaguely remembered although their attitude spoke of familiarity and entitlement.

One of the girls, her buxom physique mercilessly crushed into tight-fitting jeans and a sleeveless top, had snuggled so close to her during one of the shots that she felt her stomach heave from the overpowering smell of her perfume. The smell was something between stale fish and laundry bleach.

She must have been about twenty. *'Aunty, this your bobo fine die; una pikin dem go dey like half-caste."* she said, feigning breathlessness as she comically fanned herself with a lipstick-stained handkerchief while stealing glances at Kamsy from beneath her overly long false lashes; her admiration unabashed. *"My name na Lovina, me and Onome your sister dey like five and six."* She said it in a manner that suggested that her friendship with Àshàké's younger sister, Onome, somehow made them family.

Lovina had the brazen, rough-edged carefreeness that could only be taught by the streets. In many ways, she reminded Àshàké of her half-sister, Onome. Although they seldom spoke nor saw each other, she was her only sibling and she had hoped she would be at her wedding. When her mother informed her a week before that she hadn't seen Onome for months, she had felt that tinge of sadness and deprived longing that, for some strange reason, she associated with Aunty Iyabo's house.

"Lean a bit toward him," the photographer urged as he contorted his body to get another shot. Àshàké thought the poses the photographers requested were mostly ridiculous. But these lengthy newly-wed photo shoots have become standard at most Nigerian weddings. Then came the last shot when Kamsy had to lift her in his arms. Her ankles by then were aching from the strain of her tight heels and, despite the brief awkwardness she felt, she was glad for the respite.

Kamsy, not missing her momentary embarrassment, had given her that quizzical look that was his way of making sure she was okay. He had picked her up with ease just like he did last night and held her close; oblivious to the peals of laughter and the clicking cameras as he gazed fondly into her face, the faintest hint of a smile playing at the corners of his lips. It was a magical moment. Beyond the firm pressure of his muscular arms under her and her fingers intertwined behind his neck, she had felt a fluidity of emotions and a deep connection that went beyond vows and wedding rings.

"That was a good shot! Thanks, guys." Àshàké heard someone say, but neither of them made any attempt to let go. She was enchanted as Kamsy carried her down the chapel steps to tenderly settle her in the backseat of the Range Rover that had conveyed her and her Chief Bridesmaid to church earlier. "That's better," he breathed, as the crowd erupted in applause. They probably thought he was acting, but that was Kamsy - *her* Kamsy. When it has to do with her; tenderness, for him, came naturally.

As she wriggled her feet out of her stifling shoes, Lovina waltzed over to them visibly animated. *"Uncle, this una marriage just dey like home video. See as everybody just dey hail una,"* she said excitedly.

Like a lot of other poorly educated young Africans, the exaggerated affection and plastic romance depicted by the burgeoning African home movie industry was for her a desirable ideal. "That's how it should be," Kamsy replied, obviously amused.

In Lovina, Àshàké saw the world of her not–so–distant past. A merciless world where poverty and deprivation drove desperation and stifled potential. She could relate to the brash forwardness of this chubby teenager. It was the code for survival in a world she had known most of her life. It was a world that had conscripted her into adulthood before she had the chance to be a child.

In the blur of what should have been her childhood memories was always the little girl with the full tray of *akara* bean cakes setting out just before dawn on the long walk to the 33 Infantry Battalion Armor Depot from the cantonment mammy market to catch the night duty soldiers as they got off.

The oily balls, fried in bleached oil, provided cheap breakfast for the often-large families of the poorly paid soldiers. Though barely ten, she still remembered the parade-like precision with which she handed the soldiers the oil-soaked parcels of old newspapers as they came off the night guard duty.

This routine soon became an unofficial part of the early morning change of guard routine and the soldiers were usually nice to her. Yet, as a testimony to their sleight, her returns never tallied with her wares and Aunty Iyabo would usually exact her pound of flesh: merciless lashes on her bare back, whole days without food, and long nights kneeling on the rough cold floor behind the kitchen door.

She was jolted back to the present when she felt a tug at the top of her dress. *"Aunty, na my number be dis, make you try call me,"* Lovina was breathing into her wide-eyed face as she tucked a tiny ball of paper with a scribbled phone number into the top of her bra cup.

Àshàké's face burned with embarrassment as she watched her effortlessly elbow her way through the crowd of Kamsy's gaily dressed friends and relatives. No one seemed to have noticed but when Kamsy gently squeezed her gloved hand, she knew he had.

This unique gesture of reassurance was to become an often-needed affirmation for Àshàké as their disparate backgrounds fused in matrimony.

CHAPTER 3

The moment she sighted her mother at the solemnization service, Àshàké had immediately wished she was a bit more involved in her shopping for the occasion. Despite having sent her sixty-five thousand naira for the purpose, her mother, she realized, was a woman of fixed tastes.

If the coffee-and-cream double wrapper with the cheap 'French' lace blouse were predictable, the shimmering locally cobbled shoes were typical. *Maami* would have bought a dozen sets of those for that amount.

At the photo session, Àshàké had tried hard to ignore the dour contrast her mother and her sparse company presented to Kamsy's family - resplendent as they were in their expensive and beautifully tailored uniform *aso ebi* outfits. Despite the diversity in cut and the obvious generation–inspired differences in style, the sheer number of guests clad in the uniform cream fabric with the gold patterns spoke of what a large and well-to-do family they are.

Kamsy's mother, now the extended family matriarch since his grandmother's passing the year before, looked regal and dignified in her native outfit; an *iro* and *buba* wrapper and blouse with matching *gele* headgear - probably in solidarity with Àshàké's part-Yoruba heritage. Her high heels and Maui Jim sunglasses had added a touch of understated sophistication to her otherwise basic outfit.

Cousin after cousin came to say hello and to get introduced to Àshàké while others milled around chatting in a mixture of American-accented English and the polished diction that spoke of Nigerian top-notch private school education.

The social disparity in their backgrounds was later to be driven forcefully home to Àshàké by Buchi, Kamsy's uncle, whom she had learned ran a thriving property development firm on Lagos Island. He had walked up to them as they awaited their music cue at the main door of the reception hall with his exaggerated Idris Elba swagger and that languid self-assurance that spoke of old money.

"What is it your wife does again, Kamsy?" He asked as he took a sip from the wine glass in his hand, barely giving Àshàké a nod of acknowledgment.

After their initial visit to his exquisite apartment as part of the preliminary introduction to family members, Àshàké had wondered how he could be Kamsy's uncle seeing as he didn't look much older. That first encounter, for her, had been both disorienting and belittling.

It was not so much what he said – he had treated her with studied, almost perfect, courtesy - but it was the vibe of tolerance she felt around him. It was the same as today; he had opted to speak *about* her in her very presence, rather than speak *to* her.

'She is my personal manager; effective from today,' Kamsy had replied with a hint of uncharacteristic impatience. "Relax lil' coz, what's up with you?" Buchi said, needling him further as he smoothened Kamsy's suit lapels before sauntering away.

"I don't know why he won't keep his nose in his own business,' Kamsy was visibly miffed. It was Àshàké's turn to squeeze his hand. Thankfully, Timi Dakolo's *Iyawo mi* had defused the tension as the MC invited the guests to rise for the couple's entrance.

The reception was elaborate but lifeless. The event manager had worked extra hard to justify the three million naira Kamsy's mother paid her for the decoration of the venue. From the glittering ceiling-to-floor gold drapes that left no hint of the original walls of the auditorium, to the delicate interplay of soft gold lighting and the impeccably gold-draped tables and chairs; the hall looked like one dizzying maze of gold.

The entire ceremony wasn't any more interesting than the wedding solemnization had been; overcast as it was by the overbearing presence of the church's senior pastor, Bishop Ogene, at the special guests' table. Àshàké had wondered what the notoriously conservative aging bishop thought of all the fanfare.

She remembered their first meeting and how pleasantly surprised she had been at his impeccable dress sense. But that was as far as it went: his questions were direct and incisive; his eyes penetrating. She had the impression that he saw things that were concealed and heard things that were unsaid. Seated at the table observing the proceedings with a slightly supercilious crease to his brow, Àshàké had absent-mindedly wondered who or what it was that had displeased him.

Even Dr. Agaba, Kamsy's affable maternal uncle who chaired the reception ceremony, was unusually cautious in his remarks. A professing catholic, who only attended mass on rare occasions, Àshàké had chuckled at how he kept addressing the bishop as "My Lord Spiritual." He wasn't a man at home in religious company.

Through it all, Kamsy had looked on with detached amusement. He had given her a mischievous smirk when Mrs. Bello, the leader of the women's fellowship, in presenting her gift, spent upwards of ten minutes detailing a wife's marital roles – at least, as she understood them. "Marriage is not a bed of roses; indeed, it is not about the bed at all," she had begun to grunts of agreement from the audience comprised mostly of church members. "It is your duty as a good Christian wife to help your husband fulfill his God-ordained destiny, not just to focus on sexual pleasure." Àshàké had wondered whether the two were mutually exclusive.

When she went on to present them a gift of a beautiful outdoor baby clothes hanger, she had thought that it was either a practical joke or the women of Sanctification Chapel were in denial.

But at Sanctification Chapel, Kamsy was at home. He was a church boy and Sanctification Chapel was his spiritual habitat. He had run up and down those aisles as a toddler, sung in the children's choir, and later headed the youth ministry before leaving for medical school in Lagos.

Although time and the present demands of his surgical residency training had reduced his attendance at his home church to something of a rarity, Àshàké never ceased to wonder at how deeply, beneath the façade of his carefree playfulness, growing up in Sanctification Chapel had impacted him.

Kamsy was a kind and beautiful soul and, while she might be at odds with the foibles of a lot of these church leaders, she harbored a deep appreciation and respect for this system that gave the world, and now her, his kind.

From the perspective of her background, everything about Kamsy's life and circumstances was picture-perfect from the outset. While he had an uncanny ability to connect with her at practically every level, she could not help thinking what an effort it must be for him to relate to some of her growing-up stories. After all, his is a background of private schools, summer vacations, and doting parents.

While Kamsy's life was a predictable success; hers was an unfolding miracle.

From her earliest childhood memories growing up with Aunty Iyabo to the mess she was by the time she met him, none of these was supposed to happen. But here she was, married to this man whose love has completely overwhelmed her shame.

Several times at the wedding, just like now, she had thought she might wake up, and it would all be a dream.

SECTION

2

Predator

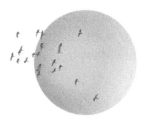

CHAPTER 4

Àshàké had no memory of how and when she came to live with Aunty Iyabo. She was therefore never able to understand why the woman seemed to have such an undisguised hatred for her. Her animosity towards her was expressed through every word and action. Even her rare and erratic acts of benevolence always had a punitive flavor.

Àshàké never forgot that Christmas - just before she turned nine. A returnee soldier from a United Nations Peace-Keeping Mission had given Aunty Iyabo a pair of shoes for Bidemi, her only daughter. Finding the shoes two sizes smaller and impossible to fit, Aunty Iyabo had asked that they be given to Àshàké, her younger cousin.

Although almost three years younger than Bidemi, Aunty Iyabo knew their shoe sizes were almost the same. Àshàké had meekly gone ahead to try them on for fear of incurring Aunty Iyabo's wrath. "Mummy, it's too tight…," she had begun, as she struggled with fitting the first leg. *"Sharrap,"* Aunty Iyabo had screamed, shaking her head from side to side like she always did before striking her with whatever was within reach. *"Se, ori e oofe nkan ti o daa.* Do you have a problem with nice things?" The coldness in her eyes had made Àshàké squeeze her feet into the shoes despite the pain and the discomfort.

On Christmas day she had worn those shoes out of dread and, along with the rest of the family, endured the almost two-kilometer trek to and from the Christmas service at the Anglican Church just opposite the Military cantonment gates. This was a once-in-a-year ritual that was the family's only pretension to religiosity.

Over a decade later, Àshàké still cringed at the painful horror she endured in the two days that followed. Aunty Iyabo had said nothing. Thankfully, Boxing Day was one of the few days in a year she didn't make her early morning rounds to the depot.

Where Àshàké was concerned, her aunt had no conscience and felt no scruples.

But the worst was yet to come.

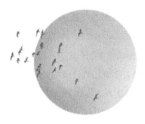

CHAPTER 5

Age thirteen came with a spurt in growth that made Àshàké's physique assume a subtle femininity that birthed a self-awareness that was, at first, unfamiliar and confusing. Lanky and fine-boned, she was already taller than most of her peers in the neighborhood. Her delicate features, accentuated by dark wavy hair, were her only legacies from a father she never knew.

Her mother had told her, on one of her rare visits to see Aunty Iyabo, how Isa, a Fulani truck driver who usually dropped off bags of onions for her on his long trips from the north to Lagos, had run out of diesel one rainy night as he arrived in their hometown.

The petroleum industry workers were yet on another of their frequent strikes and products were in short supply. As always during those times, Oba Oil, the only gas station in their small town, was shut.

Isa had sought out his usually chatty customer, whom he always assumed was married, for ideas on how to procure black-market diesel. She had instead offered him a warm meal and a bed. Their overnight liaison had resulted in Àshàké.

Isa, quite unexpectedly, never stopped by again after that night.

Even at thirteen Àshàké was street–smart enough to appreciate, in a gross kind of way, the physical transformation she was going through and the unfamiliar emotions she was experiencing. In her world, the streets taught you early and fast.

Bidemi, now fifteen, had endless stories of her escapades with boys in empty classrooms at school and with soldiers around the barrack neighborhood. She was Àshàké's self-appointed sex educator and Àshàké was a willing partaker of the goodies from her illicit enterprise. But while her stories had ignited a certain curiosity to explore her sexuality in an environment that provided ample opportunities, Àshàké deliberately avoided any male encounters. This, paradoxically, was to spite Bidemi.

Àshàké never liked her older cousin. The only child of Aunty Iyabo, Bidemi was the center of her universe. She did as she pleased and got whatever she wanted. By the time she was a high school senior, she was completely out of control.

Àshàké remembers Aunty Iyabo confronting her one day about getting home late from school. "Bibi, where are you coming from so late in the evening?" She had queried with that tentativeness that always characterized her occasional attempts at disciplining her daughter. Bidemi, rather than explain, had flown into her usual fit of tantrums and, for a whole week afterward, spoke to no one at home - except Àshàké.

Àshàké always wondered how Aunty Iyabo, despite her fiery temperament, could be so easily wrapped around her teenage daughter's little finger. She resented Bidemi for the frequent beatings she received for monies she stole, and for having to do the chores she skipped. She resented Aunty Iyabo even more for frequently venting her frustration with Bidemi on her.

So, although consumed by curiosity about Bidemi's escapades, Àshàké was adamant in her refusal to be co-opted. Bidemi's frustration at her recalcitrance gave Àshàké a strange satisfaction and a certain sense of power and revenge in a domestic relationship where everything was skewed in Bidemi's favor.

She learned to ignore the catcalls of the weed–smoking boys in the neighborhood and to avoid the groping hands of soldiers at the depot.

Sadly, with Uncle Aminu, Àshàké was unprepared.

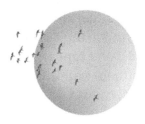

CHAPTER 6

He was the only person in their small household she could truly call a friend. It wasn't because he ever stood up for her in her various ordeals in the hands of his wife, Aunty Iyabo; no, Uncle Aminu was too much of a peace lover and wouldn't risk his wife's ire. Yet with him, she found she could share genuine laughter.

An ECOMOG peace-keeping veteran who had suffered a major hip injury from an artillery attack on his unit in Liberia, Aminu was discharged early from service on account of a major deformity. Barely thirty-two years old, and unable to process his financial benefits through the corrupt and cumbersome military bureaucracy, he had resorted to living off friends and fellow soldiers. Thankfully, the unit allowed him to retain his apartment in the Adako barracks.

Broke and with plenty of time on his hands, Aunty Iyabo's bar at the barrack mammy market soon became his favorite haunt.

What started as a convenient arrangement in which he provided his older female friend with good male company and a helping hand in exchange for hot meals and free beer, soon blossomed into a love affair.

Nobody could say for sure if or when a formal wedding took place but Aunty Iyabo soon moved in with him. Like her Aunty and older cousin, Aminu with his single crutch and howling laughter, formed a distorted background to Àshàké's childhood memories.

Àshàké remembered the cramped two-room apartment and the smell of dirt and sewage that hung so heavily around the barrack apartment blocks. There was the nightly ritual of shoving around decrepit living room furniture to create room for their raffia sleeping mats and Uncle Aminu poking them awake several times every night with his crutch as he shuffled past in between them on his multiple late-night calls to the general restrooms down the corridor.

Bidemi didn't think Uncle Aminu went to the restroom on those nights. She had told Àshàké she once spied him sneaking into D4, Corporal Yinusa's apartment.

The very amiable Corporal Yinusa was an infantryman who had been deployed to Liberia within two months of bringing home his teenage wife, Zuwera, from Kano in the north of the country. Although she was shy and spoke very little English, Zuwera was at home with the family and would often spend long hours with Uncle Aminu and Aunty Iyabo at the bar or share stories in her halting English about her siblings with Àshàké and Bidemi at the apartment.

Bidemi had confronted and pressed her about Uncle Aminu's nightly calls but Zuwera, biting her lips and dropping her gaze in that characteristic manner of hers had simply shaken her head. 'You are lying!' Bidemi had screamed at her. 'You are sleeping with him; I'll tell your husband, I'll tell everybody....' Zuwera had become visibly scared. "*Don Allah*... please, for Allah's sake," she had pleaded tearfully, the edges of her veil held tightly to her face as she always did when she was agitated.

Àshàké just stood there, helpless, as she watched her body racked by repeated sobs. "Didn't I tell you?" Bidemi was gleeful as she turned to Àshàké. There was that triumphant glint in her eyes she always had when things went her way – which was often.

Àshàké initially dismissed Bidemi's story about Zuwera and Uncle Aminu as part of her usual mischief-making. After all, Corporal Yinusa and Uncle Aminu were good friends and he was like a father to Zuwera, just like he was to them both.

Uncle Aminu was helpful, playful, and very funny.

On Saturday mornings, when he stayed home to do his and Aunty Iyabo's laundry, he would laugh and chase Àshàké around as he tried to put large mounds of soap lather on her wavy hair.

Bidemi never played with Uncle Aminu. She never called or referred to him as Dad. There was a coldness between them that Àshàké found deeply mysterious. As she grew older, she also noticed Aunty Iyabo was wary of him around Bidemi.

Àshàké could not recall Uncle Aminu ever being alone with Bidemi. There seemed to be a tacit agreement between him and Aunty Iyabo that he never should, though nobody ever mentioned why. Even Bidemi, who relished sharing people's secrets, never talked about it; so Àshàké never asked.

One morning, about the time Bidemi turned fifteen, she had come down with a severe fever and had to stay home. Uncle Aminu, in his usual good-natured manner, had offered to stay home and look after her. "You can go to the bar. I'll wait to make sure she is okay," he told Aunty Iyabo.

Aunty Iyabo's reaction was instantaneous. *"You are a liar! Iro ni!* It won't happen again, never again!" Àshàké had watched, perplexed, as Uncle Aminu just stood there swallowing nervously; his prominent Adam's apple moving up and down like a lump of inexpressible hurt lodged in his throat. As Aunty Iyabo pranced around clapping her hands in his face, Àshàké had thought for a moment she would slap him. All through the drama, Bidemi just sat there, a distant look in her tear-brimmed eyes.

Àshàké eventually had to miss school to stay home with her.

Bidemi was the strong one, but that morning she had looked so vulnerable; almost distraught. Beyond the discomfort of her fever, something in that morning's exchange had deeply troubled her. Something only the three of them knew. Àshàké was consumed with curiosity and resolved to find out why Uncle Aminu should not stay home to care for his daughter and what it was that *must not happen again.* So, she asked her.

'Nothing,' was her curt reply as she looked away, once again lost in her thoughts. It was to be almost two years later before it all finally made sense.

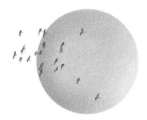

CHAPTER 7

As Àshàké began to blossom into early womanhood, her relationship with Uncle Aminu seemed to evolve. At first, the frequent and unnecessary body contacts were subtle and she thought it was all part of his usual playfulness. But it was as if words were never enough... no matter what he wanted to say to her; Uncle Aminu would always touch her.

With time, the little pats and playful pinches progressed to frequent groping of her bottom and chest. He seemed obsessed with details of her budding sexuality; always asking uncomfortable questions and making gross and embarrassing remarks. Even the most ordinary conversations became laced with sexual nuances.

Then came that Friday afternoon in August.

She had come home early from school as is usual on Fridays. Finding the doors locked and thinking no one was home, she had let herself in through the kitchen door with the single key she shared with Bidemi. After removing her shirt and skirt in the kitchen, she had dropped them in the large plastic bucket they used for their school laundry. Pausing momentarily, she perfunctorily took in her upper torso in the plastic-framed mirror that hung on the wall of what should have been the dining area of the house where Aunty Iyabo now stacked her crates of beer.

Àshàké always worried about the size of her breasts. Although people always told her how much prettier than Bidemi she was, she always wished her breasts were as big as hers.

One day as she was helping Uncle Aminu wash some used beer glasses at the bar, he had said to Aunty Iyabo – out of the blues and a bit too loudly, 'I think Àshàké will need brassieres too." Àshàké had, on self-conscious instinct, turned away from him and adjusted her loose top. "*Abeg! Wetin she wan put inside bra?*" Aunty Iyabo had retorted, her voice dripping with disdain.

Àshàké felt humiliated at the sound of muffled laughter as the mostly inebriated soldiers at the bar all simultaneously turned to look at her chest as if to confirm that she actually had nothing to put in a bra.

In the subsequent year or two, Àshàké's breasts had become fuller and even slightly pendulous, but Aunty Iyabo never bought her a bra.

She had nearly four hours to kill before Bidemi got home and they would have to set out to assist Aunty Iyabo and Uncle Aminu at the bar. Àshàké had looked forward to watching some of the new African movies Uncle Aminu just added to his collection, but as she neared the block, the sputtering sound of the stand-by power generator from the barber's kiosk announced to her that it was not to be. Power was out again.

The living room was stuffy. That distinct tobacco-like smell that always seemed to follow Uncle Aminu hung heavily in the air. Bidemi always claimed he smoked though no one in the house had ever actually seen him with a cigarette. Àshàké thought it came from the heavy cloud of cigarette smoke he was constantly immersed in at the bar. *Passive smoking,* she remembered the Health Science teacher called it. Everyone in the house probably smelled of tobacco in some way.

She had almost reached her room door when she froze. Silence. But she was sure she heard something move. Someone was in the sitting room. Instinctively she crossed her arms on her bare chest as her mouth widened into an inaudible scream. "Àshàké, it's me." The voice sounded strangely husky and shaky, but it was Uncle Aminu.

She turned her head towards him, careful neither to turn her back nor front towards him in her semi-nudity. He was standing within reach of her. *He didn't have his crutch!*

"G-good afternoon, Uncle," she blurted out, as she dashed for the room. "Wait..." he said, his tone slightly commanding as his sweaty right hand shot out and took hold of her bare upper arm; his blunt fingernails digging into her flesh. Àshàké's eyes were, by now, wild with fright. Uncle Aminu looked different. His face glistened with tiny beads of sweat in the dim light and his eyes were like chips of glass. He was scary.

"I didn't want to do this...," he said in a barely audible whisper. Then he seemed to hesitate. "Àshàké. You know you are like my daughter...," he said, slightly loosening his grip on her arm. Àshàké just stood there, too terrified to move or scream. Her mouth was momentarily dry; the pounding in her chest audible in her ears.

Then as if propelled by an overwhelming force he was all over her; his powerful arms grabbing her around the midriff and violently yanking her off her feet. She kicked and thrashed wildly as she fruitlessly tried to grab the doorpost. But her strength was no match for the trained soldier.

Everything passed in a terrifying blur: The sandy roughness of the mattress on her face as she struggled to breathe, his vice-like grip around the back of her neck, and the shafts of pain that shot through her body as he viciously ripped through her innocence. The pains gradually gave way to light-headedness, then darkness as she blacked out.

It probably lasted a few minutes, but it felt like an eternity. Uncle Aminu had unceremoniously crashed her into womanhood and, in the process, shattered all her teenage romantic fantasies. There had been no songs, no hands held, no sweet words spoken.

The only person she called friend, in a world where nobody appeared to want her, had violently snatched her innocence without so much as acknowledging her humanness.

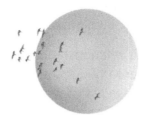

CHAPTER 8

Àshàké! Àshàké! Someone was calling her.

Even in her grogginess, she could recognize the voice. It was Bidemi. Her voice sounded faint and distant. She tried to open her eyes. Her face was wet and slimy and her eyes stung. From the bitter taste in her mouth, she knew she was laying in her own vomit. "Àshàké, open your eyes," Bidemi said, trying to turn her over. Her neck hurt and her legs felt numb. "Can you hear me? Àshàké, wake up..."

Bidemi was frantic as she lifted her school skirt to wipe the slime from Àshàké's face. "Bibi, what happened?" she asked as Bidemi's alarmed face floated into focus. And almost simultaneously, it hit her. Despite the excruciating pains she felt, she sat bolt upright on the bed, her eyes alarmed as she stared down at her naked thighs, her tears beginning to flow freely as she looked up at Bidemi.

"It was him," Bidemi said. Her voice had a sad knowingness to it; as if to dispel any lingering hope that, maybe, the soreness Àshàké felt had some other plausible explanation. "He did it to me too," she said as she began to sob. She was holding her skirt so tightly in her clenched fists that her knuckles shone.

Then it all suddenly made sense to Àshàké. Poor Bidemi!

Àshàké, felt a bursting dam of mixed emotions as she reached out and held Bidemi close; pressing her now wet cheek to her naked shoulder. It was like holding a little sister as Bidemi clung tightly to her as if to draw on some hidden strength. Completely overcome by her disclosure, Àshàké suddenly didn't care about her own ordeal anymore.

That moment redefined their relationship. Àshàké felt every resentment she previously felt towards her rambunctious cousin melt away. They were no longer teenagers pitched against each other by a mother's favoritism but two women united in their shared experience of the unbridled lust and savage assault of one man.

'Does Aunty Know?' Àshàké asked as she let go of Bidemi to wipe her body with the soiled bed sheet. "The first time," she said, catching her breath in between sobs. She looked so small and forlorn, and Àshàké felt an overwhelming urge to protect her. "She threatened to report him to the Regimental Sergeant Major, but he begged and begged, promising it would not happen again..." "And he never stopped?" Àshàké interjected. She nodded lightly; her head bowed as she nervously fiddled with a local leather bracelet on her left wrist.

"And he is not my father." She said, momentarily raising her head to look at Àshàké. "Uncle Aminu is not your father?" Àshàké was surprised. Bidemi nodded as she turned to look out of the window at the vast undulating landscape of Adako Barracks with its rows of residential blocks.

Backdrop

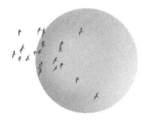

CHAPTER 9

Iyabo's marriage to Idowu was blissful but short-lived.

In the turbulent early two thousands when the military held sway in national politics, Idowu was the typical privileged soldier: ruthless, rich, and corrupt. A notable marksman who had earned special recognition from the Army Chief for gallantry during his brief stint with the ECOMOG forces in Liberia, he had on his return been adopted by Colonel Davies, the commanding officer of the 33rd infantry, as an unofficial 'super batsman.'

Tough and streetwise, he was recognized as CO's "man on the ground' amongst the troops that provided security cover for the massive Otete Petroleum Products Loading Depot that served the major commercial cities in the Southwest. Idowu ran everything for Colonel Davies; from receiving and disposing of the unofficial daily allocation of a thirty-three-thousand-liter truckload of petrol allocated to the regiment - ostensibly 'to aid logistics,' to ensuring accurate returns to the CO of the huge toll extorted from petroleum tanker drivers by the troops to facilitate their access to the congested loading points.

Within a year of his return from his tour of duty in Liberia, Idowu had become a man of considerable means. Reputed for his many SUVs and immaculate Kaftans, he was the untouchable boss's right-hand man whom his superiors resented but didn't dare tangle with.

A kind man at heart, Idowu was generous with his wealth and influence. Whether it was assisting a soldier's wife in distress or putting in a word for a fellow soldier in need; he always tried to help.

Unlike most of his colleagues in the army, Idowu had no women and drank no alcohol. But whenever it was required – which was often – he ensured the regimental guest house, tucked away behind well-trimmed hedges and tall trees in the posh Government Reservation Area of the city, was furnished with liquor and women for his Commanding Officer and his unending stream of raucous military and civilian guests.

Mrs. Davies liked Idowu and considered him a good moral influence on her husband. "ID, don't allow all those slender girls get their claws on my husband *o*," she would often plead in her deeply accented English. "Not when Idowu is in charge, Madam," he would say, laughing.

She was a good-natured woman with average education and Idowu always found her naivety amusing. She was barely eighteen when she married the young Lieutenant Davies just freshly graduated from the military academy. Her father, who had retired from the army as a master warrant officer, had never hidden his desire for his only daughter to marry an officer.

Colonel Davies, in so many ways, was a dream come true for her family. Well-liked amongst his superiors, he had, from the early years of the junta, headed several 'juicy' government task forces and made stupendous amounts of illicit wealth. These he had generously translated into relative affluence for his aging father-in-law and a very good life for Mrs. Davies and their four sons.

It was part of Idowu's duty to keep Mrs. Davies comfortable within the confines of the simple world her husband had created. A world in which her prayers and frequent church attendance were responsible for the favor he enjoyed and the wealth he had acquired. Although Colonel Davies hardly ever attended either of the Catholic or Protestant Chapels in the barracks - except for occasional official ceremonies, she still thought him a shining example of Christian virtue and always told him so.

The thought of her husband's numerous affairs and riotous lifestyle would have sounded far-fetched to Mrs. Davies, so, although Idowu often pitied her, he kept her blissfully uninformed, and the home front at peace.

When Mrs. Davies called Idowu one Sunday afternoon to inform him about her decision to get a grown-up live-in maid to help with her boys; he had immediately swung into action deploying his extensive contacts in the city and within the barrack community in search of a suitable person. He was familiar enough with Mrs. Davies and the internal workings of the Davies household to know exactly what was required.

To his surprise, it had turned out to be a more difficult task than he imagined as he tried to balance the pros and cons of the several candidates directed to him. A man of precision and used to being on target, he had begun to doubt his competence to deliver on the task when the barman at the officers' mess called him to say he had a distant older cousin who would be suitable to assist the CO's wife.

Cynical and near frustrated, he had decided to give the interviews one last shot.

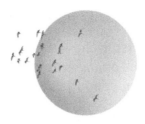

CHAPTER 10

Iyabo was different.

Dark-skinned, voluptuous, and standing at just slightly over five feet tall; there was a briskness in her mannerism that hinted at impatience. When they eventually met, her gaze was steady; her attitude, sure. Idowu was well–known and had no doubt that she, at least, had heard about him; yet, she managed to come across as polite but unimpressed.

"Are you sure you can do the job," Idowu had asked, finally.

In that distracted, almost impatient tone, she had replied, "is it not to look after little children, *what's there*?" Then, as if to ensure they were on the same page, she said, "I hope your madam doesn't shout at people *sha*." Her tone was almost taunting as she said, *'your Madam...'*

There was a depth - a mystery - about this chubby, barely educated young woman in the cheap flowery dress that Idowu wanted to explore.

Madam had her maid!

The love chemistry between Iyabo and Idowu was initially awkward but they found an unlikely enabler in Mrs. Davies. Although she had found Iyabo to be an excellent warden for the boys and an efficient housekeeper, her brashness was a major put-off. But if she, of all women, was the one that caught Idowu's fancy, Mrs. Davies was more than willing to shelve her reservations.

It turned out to be a whirlwind romance between two unlikely lovebirds and by February of that year, they were wed at the Regimental Protestant Chapel with Colonel and Mrs. Davies standing in as the bride's parents.

Idowu had immediately settled Iyabo into a nicely furnished apartment in the city; well away from the prying eyes of the barrack community and her life soon assumed an easy, comfortable rhythm.

This was to be disrupted, after a few months, by a continuous stream of clandestine visitors, including Colonel Davies and other unfamiliar officers, to the apartment. Iyabo attributed this to Idowu's business involvement with CO although that didn't explain why they would always huddle together speaking in hushed tones. She was to know soon enough.

It was a wet morning on August 15th, exactly six months after they were wed. She had been feeling crippling bouts of lower abdominal pain for over a week but would swallow some of the aspirins Idowu left around the house whenever it got unbearable. She hoped Idowu would soon be home to take her to see his doctor at the specialist hospital in town but he had been gone for over two weeks; only calling occasionally to make sure she was okay.

He never offered any explanations as to his whereabouts.

'ID, what's happening?' She had ventured the day before. "Work." was his curt reply. Then, as if on second thoughts, he had softened, "sorry, I'm just stressed... I'll call you." The phone had gone dead. There was something unusual about the tension in his voice. He didn't appear to have heard anything she said about the cramps she was having so when the waves of nausea began, she decided to board a tricycle and go to the medical inspection room in the barracks.

The matron had immediately recognized her. *"Iyawo Idowu ti loyun;* Idowu's wife is pregnant," she announced, animated. "Matron, I am not pregnant *o,*" Iyabo protested, managing a weak smile. But the matron would have none of that.

She had immediately thrust a plastic bottle into her hand and pointed her to the bathroom. When the matron emerged from the side lab a few minutes later with a broad smile on her face, Iyabo knew immediately. The cramps, nausea, sleepiness; everything suddenly made sense.

Later, as the tiny particulars of the new life that was forming in her were demonstrated to her on ultrasound, her eyes filled with tears. She was going to have Idowu's baby and she couldn't wait to tell him.

All the way home, she kept calling him but couldn't reach his phone. When he hadn't called by 4 pm that day, her excitement became laced with anxiety and a certain sense of foreboding. She had later fallen into an exhausted sleep with her right hand still clutching the ultrasound report.

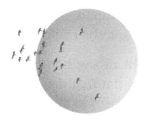

CHAPTER 11

Idowu was rubbing her protruding tummy, pressing his ears to it, tickling her.

She was trying to ask him where he had been but he kept laughing, never raising his head. Then she felt blood running down her thighs. *Somebody was bleeding. Was she losing the baby?* But still, he didn't raise his head. The blood was now forming a puddle around her feet. "ID, look up...." she kept saying, but he had become still, his clean-shaven head cold as a block of ice.

The scream rising from her throat was interrupted by a loud crashing noise from the sitting room and the sound of neighbors shouting.

She was still clutching the test result when she woke up, her heart racing. As she ran into the expansive sitting room, she met fierce-looking, unfamiliar soldiers ransacking drawers and turning over furniture.

The central glass pane in the front door was shattered and she could feel fine pieces of glass prick her bare feet as she walked in trembling. 'Where is Sergeant Idowu?' the young captain that led them had barked at her. 'He has been at the loading depot for the past two weeks, Sir,' she said, her hands on her mouth.

The soldiers had exchanged glances and as if on cue, had turned and left without uttering another word.

Within minutes Iyabo was on the phone. She called Idowu, Mrs. Davies, and finally Col. Davies: but nobody answered. She only began to make sense of what was going on when Musa, the CO's talkative batsman, called her about half an hour later. "Iyabo, they have taken away *Oga* Idowu and CO," he said, his voice hollow with fear. "Taken them away? Where?" she queried, momentarily irritated.

How long would it take Musa to wake up to the reality of her new status as Mrs. Maxwell Idowu? *The boy needed to be taught a lesson.* She was making a mental note to tell Idowu he had called her *Iyabo* again but his next words had frozen her to her heart: "Iyabo..., there has been a coup, switch on the radio...." then the phone went dead.

By the time the dust settled about four days later, the coup had failed. Thirty-one officers and men were found guilty of treason by the special military court and were summarily executed. Iyabo was a pregnant widow.

The months that followed were harrowing as the regime was methodical and thorough in erasing, not just the mutinous soldiers, but their careers as well. Jobless, and with no spousal gratuity to fall back on, Iyabo began her long tortuous journey through homelessness, single motherhood and abject poverty, to eventual survival.

Àshàké was completely enthralled as she listened to Bidemi tell her version of the story of her parenting. 'Mummy told me my dad always gave money to Uncle Aminu,' she said in a pained tone of voice. 'He was the one that begged the CO to leave him in his apartment after his forced retirement.' Àshàké was nodding. Everything was coming together.

"Uncle Aminu is evil. I will tell Aunty Iyabo what he did to me," she said, wincing in pain, as she stood up and reached for the torn brown towel they both shared.

Bidemi said nothing.

Defiance

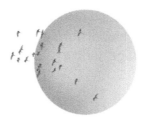

CHAPTER 12

The rhythmic thudding sound of Uncle Aminu's crutch on the stairs outside announced their return from the bar. Bidemi had fallen asleep on the bed where she had left her and Àshàké was sprawled on the old settee in the sitting room.

She would normally have run out to help with whatever bags or empty beer crates they were carrying, but she ached all over, and just walking down the steep stairs would have been an ordeal. She also felt something else: indifference.

The events of the previous six hours had changed her in a very strange way. She understood Aunty Iyabo better and, in so doing, had lost all fear of her. She resented her for marrying Uncle Aminu and for the things he had done to Bidemi, and, now, to her.

"Àshàké!" Aunty Iyabo's voice was raspy and Àshàké knew what was coming. Still, she didn't care. She just lay there. Waiting. It was Uncle Aminu that switched on the lights. Aunty Iyabo was just behind him, breathless from hauling an empty crate of beer up the two flights of stairs. Something about Àshàké lying there on the couch seemed to tick her off.

"You are here sleeping while I'm out slaving for you?" She screamed, carelessly tossing aside the crate. Uncle Aminu was about to say something to Àshàké when Aunty Iyabo pushed past him; charging towards her with a leather slipper in hand. She was all over her before she had the chance to sit up.

As the blows began to land all over her face, Àshàké tried unsuccessfully to fend her off. Her eyes were beginning to sting with tears and she could taste the warm saltiness of blood from a broken lip; but Aunty Iyabo, completely consumed with rage, didn't let up.

It was all Àshàké could take.

With all the strength she could muster, she had drawn up her thighs flat on her chest and kicked, propelling Aunty Iyabo across the room with both feet, and sending her chubby frame hurtling across the room and crashing into the large rickety shelf that held their old TV set. The shelf and its contents came crashing down on her as she hit the floor with a sickening thud before going perfectly still. Uncle Aminu stood as if transfixed in the open doorway.

Àshàké rose slowly off the couch, wiping blood off her lips with the back of her hand as Bidemi ran in, kneeling by the shelf and screaming at a bemused Uncle Aminu, "come and help her! This was all your fault!"

There were sounds of running feet in the corridor and a few seconds later, the small sitting room was full of people. "Ah! Aunty mi ti ku, she is dead" Mama Simi, their quarrelsome neighbor that sold corn pap downstairs kept screaming as she stared down in horror at the twisted body of Aunty Iyabo, both hands on her head. "Stop it! She is not dead, she only fainted," someone else tried to console her from within the small crowd. Several others got busy applying native resuscitation techniques to revive her; splashing water on her face and forcing a metal spoon in between her teeth.

The ambulance and the Regimental Police arrived almost simultaneously. As the Regimental Police officers led Àshàké away, she could see the small pool of blood on the floor from where the army medics had picked up Aunty Iyabo's limp body a few minutes earlier. She had been so still that Àshàké had wondered whether she was dead. Yet, strangely, she felt nothing. No remorse, no sympathy.

Benefactor

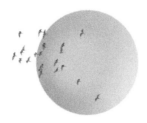

CHAPTER 13

Captain Faruk was notorious for women and had a reputation for ruthlessness amongst the residents of the barracks community.

As adjutant of the 33rd Infantry, his office was the court of final arbitration for all cases of discipline for soldiers and conflict between civilians in the barracks. His superiors gave him all the leeway he needed to keep everyone in line; a task he performed creditably well.

He occasionally stopped by at the bar whenever he visited the mammy market in the course of work and Àshàké always marveled at how everyone was on their best behavior around him.

It was 7.40 pm when the RPs brought Àshàké to his house. He had come out on the balcony clad in a long white robe, with a white towel draped on his neck. After listening to their report, he looked at Àshàké and asked, 'How old are you?' "Fifteen," she mumbled, pulling her partly torn dress around her.

After looking her over for a while, as if trying to decide what to do with her, he called his batsman and, tossing him a bunch of keys, said, "Take her to the MIR and let them clean up those wounds and bring her back immediately." "Yes, Sir," he saluted and immediately drove her to the medical inspection room.

As they drove in silence to the MIR, Àshàké could sense that her life was about to change. But little did she know just how drastic that change was going to be. While her stay with Aunty Iyabo was abusive, it had provided her with the structure and stability she needed growing up. The early childhood years spent with her mother in Ajagun had become faint unconnected patches of memory. Aunty Iyabo and her family were the only family she knew.

As the doctor picked the ragged edges of her broken lips with small forceps and sewed them together with tiny blue sutures, her mind kept wandering to Aunty Iyabo and the grotesque way her head had lain beneath the shelf. For a fleeting moment, she wondered if she was dead, but had immediately pushed the thought away.

She was later to learn from the attending nurse that Aunty Iyabo had been transferred to the ICU of the military hospital. Again, she couldn't get herself to feel sorry for her.

She also wondered about Bidemi. She surely must hate her now. After all, Aunty Iyabo was her mother.

Àshàké hadn't known what to expect as she was returned to Captain Faruk's house. The pain from her stitched lips was getting worse and her head was pounding. The doctor had given her the same red pills they normally gave her for cramps during her periods and, though she longed for water to swallow them to ease the pains, she had even bigger concerns.

Deep down she feared Captain Faruk might send her to the civilian women's guardroom where, as she heard, grown-ups peed on the floor and eased themselves in potties. They might even send her to prison if Aunty Iyabo died. She shuddered.

Captain Faruk was surprisingly nice. He had offered her a can of coke and some doughnuts and patiently listened to her story. Àshàké had narrated her ordeal at home and how it culminated in what happened that afternoon. She did not mention the incident with Uncle Aminu.

In the end, he dismissed the RPs and handed her over to Fatima, his housekeeper. "Fati, this girl has been through a lot," he said, "make her as comfortable as possible till I see CO tomorrow." Fatima had swung into action immediately. Within an hour, Àshàké was sitting in front of the wide TV screen in the family lounge clad in clean pajamas. "It belongs to Jamila," Fatima had informed her as she pulled the pajamas and other girl clothes out of one of the drawers in a chest inside a beautiful bedroom with pink and sky-blue walls.

As Àshàké peered at the gold-framed family photograph on the wall of the lounge, Fatima explained that Mrs. Faruk and her children; Jamila and Bala, were in Jos from where captain Faruk was transferred to the 33rd infantry. He had bought a house and settled them in the temperate north-central city to avoid disruptions to the children's school occasioned by his frequent redeployments.

Jamila's face in the photo was dark and pretty with clear bright eyes and Àshàké wondered what she would think of her wearing her clothes and sleeping in her bed.

Captain Faruk informed Àshàké the next morning that her aunt was taken for emergency surgery the night before and that she was in stable condition. She was glad Aunty Iyabo was alive though that seemed to increase the uncertainties surrounding her own fate. The CO in the meantime had ordered that she remain in Captain Faruk's house until Aunty Iyabo's discharge from the hospital and Fatima had gone ahead to settle her in.

The house chores were basic but Fatima hardly let her help. "*Oga* said you are here to rest," she would say whenever Àshàké tried to help out. Though Àshàké had heard and even read about washing machines, she was fascinated to actually see one in operation. The first day Fatima put her blood-stained dress in the machine she was sure the turning drum wasn't going to make her dress clean and she had told her so. Fatima had smiled patiently and simply told her, "Wait and see." To her delight, it had not only come out clean but dry as well.

Àshàké enjoyed the shower in Jamila's room. She liked the tingling sensation from the tiny jets of the high-pressure hand shower as she directed it at different parts of her body. She would gradually turn the tap handle left till the water temperature began to sting and then suddenly turn it all the way right. She liked to watch the goose pimples cover her skin as the cold jets returned.

It was so unlike home where Aunty Iyabo would send her to buy waste wood from Jamiu the carpenter's shed to make fire, especially in the harmattan, to warm up bath water for everyone. They never used the single-burner camp gas cooker for bath water. Aunty Iyabo guarded the gas jealously.

The bathroom quickly became Àshàké's favorite place in the house and she was there three times a day. *"Mami Wata,"* Fatima called her one day as she dried her hair with a towel in front of the full-length mirror in the narrow hallway after one of her long showers. Àshàké had felt strangely elated that Fatima thought her as beautiful as the mythical African water spirit.

On impulse, she held open the larger towel tied around her chest to briefly inspect the frontal nudity of her slim but well-rounded fifteen-year-old body. Fatima was right, she *was* beautiful.

In some way, she felt somewhat liberated in the few days she had spent in this large, very well-kept house with its seeming abundance of everything. The constantly humming deep freezer in the kitchen was stocked with assorted meats, snails, and shrimps and Àshàké wondered how just two persons could have so much to eat. *"Oga* Faruk doesn't eat sugar," Fatima had informed her earlier. Yet, the fridge was filled with an assortment of beers and juices. Fatima took her meal requests thrice a day and in between, she helped herself to whatever fruits or drinks she wanted.

It had only been a few days and, though Àshàké couldn't say exactly when, something was changing in her, and fast. This was a life she had heard existed but could not have envisioned. Now she was living it. She could hardly imagine herself living any other way. She would daydream of Jamila and Bala visiting and the three of them sitting on the beautifully patterned rug, watching TV together. She wondered if Jamila would like her; whether they would both sleep in her bed.

Although she seldom saw Captain Faruk, she liked him and looked forward to his brief appearances at home in the evenings. He would sit briefly on the L–shaped couch in the lounge, drink his glass of water, and then he was off again to attend to some issue for the CO or spend time with colleagues at the officers' mess.

He would often ask what she ate or drank, or what she watched on TV. Àshàké liked his clean hairless face and the way his lips seemed to speak and smile all at once. He wasn't anything like uncle Aminu with his rough hairy face and tobacco stench.

Captain Faruk was never home when Àshàké went to bed but she knew he always looked into her room before retiring to bed. The grating sound of tires on the loose granite chippings in the driveway would usually wake her up as he drove in. She would follow his every movement with her ears as he went through his bedtime routine: the brief sound of the TV as he switched it on and then off, the sound of shifting bottles as he rummaged in the fridge for a bottle of water and the inevitable phone call to his wife.

Even through her shut door, Àshàké could often pick up the hint of impatience in his voice whenever he spoke with her. Although she never did hear the other end of their conversation, Àshàké thought his tone often spoke of frustration and deep unhappiness. "*Mai ki kai so,* Jumai? What do you want from me?" Àshàké once heard him ask in a harsh whisper.

She longed to ask him why they always fought on the phone; to say something that would make him feel better. When her door finally opened and the shadowy outline of his tall frame appeared in the doorway, she would know he was about to go to bed.

She would pretend to be asleep as she watched him; his usually topless silhouette filling the doorway. He would then gently shut the door again before entering his bedroom next door.

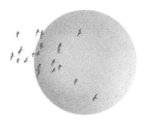

CHAPTER 14

Tom and Jerry were up to their usual cat-and-mouse games and Àshàké, sitting on the rug in Jamila's cream nightie, was completely absorbed in front of the TV screen as she absent-mindedly tried to weave her lush black hair into large braids.

Mama Kudi, Aunty Iyabo's friend from block 6, always enjoyed helping her plait it with black cotton threads on Saturday evenings but since she came to Captain Faruk's house, she would simply divide it down the middle and make two large braids.

Àshàké hadn't heard the car in the driveway, nor did she hear Captain Faruk walk in. "Àshàké, go and get dressed, the CO wants to see you." She had swung around startled, instinctively crossing her arms across her chest, clasping both shoulders with her hands. "Yes, Sir," she muttered as she turned again to stare blankly at the TV screen. She didn't move.

Jamila's nightgown was way too short for her and she wished she had tied a wrapper on it. It felt awkward sitting there but she couldn't walk across the room so scantily clad – not with him standing there.

Captain Faruk didn't move either. He just stood there looking strong and authoritative in his crisp army camouflage; his left hand on the doorknob, his face contemplative. It was as if he was trying to decide whether to come in or to wait outside. They were alone in the house, but she wasn't afraid; just embarrassed.

He came in.

Walking casually to the fridge, he took a bottle of water and took his time selecting a glass from the door rack - all the while making sure his back was fully turned to her. Àshàké caught the hint. "Yes, sir," she said again as she bolted out of the room.

The short drive to the regimental headquarters was quiet. Àshàké was dressed in another of Jamila's clothes; a simple lemon-green sweatshirt and a pair of jeans with a hem almost two inches shy of her ankles. Captain Faruk appeared completely relaxed, the hint of a smile back on his smooth face, his two hands stretched out and firmly holding the steering wheel close to the top. Àshàké thought he looked happy and wondered why.

An orderly met them as they drove into the small parking lot. "Take her to CO's office," Captain Faruk said curtly. "Yes, sir," saluted the soldier. A single wide tribal mark ran down the side of his dark face; from near the bridge of his nose down to the right margin of his mouth. Àshàké wondered what tribe he was, maybe *Ebira*. "Follow me," the soldier said, motioning to her.

The CO rose from behind his wide cluttered desk as she was ushered in. "Àshàké, why didn't you tell me about Aminu?" He asked, his tone ominous with suppressed anger. "You girls let that bastard abuse you and you kept quiet?" Àshàké's mind was racing. *Who told him? How did he know about Bidemi?*

"He only did it to her once," Bidemi's voice was quiet and subdued. Àshàké hadn't noticed her sitting on the sofa behind the open door, facing the CO's table. "Bi-bi…" she began, surprised and suddenly overwhelmed by a deluge of confusing emotions.

Bidemi looked drawn, poor, and unkempt. Her short, dark green suede dress, which Àshàké used to admire just a few weeks before, now looked odd and out of place in this expansive office with its multiple flags and authoritative air. Àshàké felt a pang of guilt at not having thought of her much in the past two weeks. In the excitement of her new life, Bidemi had scarcely crossed her mind.

"Bibi, I'm so sorry," she said, tugging at the sleeves of her sweatshirt as if the stark contrast in their clothes was her crime. "Young lady, the commanding officer is talking to you!" The orderly snapped, a hint of studied impatience in his voice, but the CO waved him to silence. He was engrossed in the moment; his expression heavy with compassion. All his initial anger at them had melted away as he watched, captivated by these two teenage girls, and the unfolding poignant drama surrounding their young lives.

While Àshàké had felt a pang of guilt and deep pity at seeing her older cousin, she had also realized how much she now abhorred the life she represented. She resolved that, no matter what happened, she wasn't going back to Aunty Iyabo's house.

"Take the bastard inside!" It was Captain Faruk. When the door opened, two soldiers brought in Uncle Aminu, both feet scraping the floor as they tried to hold up his tall frame between them. His usual tobacco stench was now overshadowed by the strong acrid smell of urine. Àshàké had smelled him before she saw him. He had patches of dry blood all over his face and his eyes had a dull quality to them. He appeared to be struggling to focus and Àshàké could tell he wanted to say something to her.

When the soldiers let him go, he had crumbled into a pitiful heap on the floor. Àshàké noticed his right foot was bloody and disfigured as if someone had crushed it with a heavy object. Her stomach began to heave as she felt a rush of saliva filling her mouth. She could hear the CO's fading voice say, "My friend, you are on your way to jail..." She tried to reach for the doorknob to break her fall; then she passed out.

She woke up in the hospital to the sound of Fatima's voice. "She is awake!" she exclaimed. Àshàké could make out multiple blurry faces as she tried to open her eyes. "You are in hospital," a nurse informed her as she wrapped a blood pressure cuff around her arm. "You passed out but you are okay now," she said a few minutes later as she unwrapped the cuff and walked away.

Fatima was sitting by her bed, a deeply worried look on her face. "*Oga* Faruk said he'll come and take you home in the evening." Àshàké raised her hand to touch a sore slightly swollen area on her left temple. She was about to ask about Bidemi and Uncle Aminu but she still felt very weak.

In a few minutes, she had drifted into a troubled sleep.

She was standing outside an open door. There was the sound of crying coming from the darkness within. It was a woman. Àshàké went down on all fours, peering into the room to see who it is that was so distressed. She could make out the shadowy figure of Aunty Iyabo on the floor her hand and legs moving continuously as she trashed around. But the voice was not hers.

Then the soldiers were pulling her up; putting shackles on her wrists. Àshàké was resisting; screaming and kicking...

Someone was tapping her shoulder. It was Aunty Fati. "Wake up, Àshàké... wake up!" She took her in her soothing embrace. Then she was fast asleep again.

Boundless

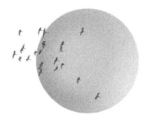

CHAPTER 15

Àshàké had had a very stormy night. That note from Faruk had deeply unsettled her. All night she kept fending off a feeling of suffocating fear that kept trying to envelop her. Even after having a cold glass of milk, it had taken hours for sleep to finally overtake her.

In the morning, as she stepped out of Nandi Hall, her watch said 7.52 am. The morning air was crisp, even a bit chilly. The lush green of the campus grounds stretched in all directions. She was running late again. Àshàké always found the scenic beauty of Idris Johnson Abubakar University breathtaking. The vast undulating lawns formed huge ripples of vibrant green as they merged with the mounds of small hills in the distance.

The recently mowed *erysopogum*, wet with the early harmattan dew, shone as the first rays of the sun broke through the harmattan fog. "Pearl on the plateau" was indeed a fitting sobriquet for Idris Johnson Abubakar University.

She had only eight minutes and she needed approximately twelve if she was to make the sociology 301 class on time. Dr. Zazi, a stickler for punctuality, hadn't been a little displeased at her lateness just two days before and he had made no attempt to be pleasant in communicating it to her - and the rest of the class. "Young lady, let this first time be the last time I get here before you," he growled. "The rest of you will do well to take note." There was no voiced threat of consequence, but everyone had gotten the message. Showing up late for the second consecutive time, therefore, was out of the question.

She was grateful for the distraction that making it to class on time provided. That way she had a momentary respite from her preoccupation with Faruk's health and the far-reaching implications of the worst-case scenario. She shivered; more from her anxiety than from the harmattan chill.

Ignoring the "Keep off the Lawns" sign by the walkway, she made a beeline for the wide quadrangle in front of lecture hall 6, silently praying that none of the ubiquitous gardeners from Lawn Care would sight her walking on the greens. While Àshàké loved the gardens and parks of Johnson, she was never able to understand the gardeners' exaggerated emotional reaction to 'trespassers.'

Her feet were becoming damp as the moisture began to gradually saturate the khaki fabric of her tennis shoes.

It was eight o'clock when she passed by the twelve-foot burnished brass statue of the university's namesake at the middle of the Founders' Quadrangle. The masterful depiction of Johnson Idris Abubakar in full academic regalia; a bowl of assorted fruits in hand, seemed to capture the cultural and academic essence of the university while conferring a picturesque ambience on the otherwise barren expanse of the Quadrangle.

She broke into a trot. If Dr. Zazi was already in class, her day was about to start off worse than her night.

Kal was waving and beckoning to her from the back as she stood momentarily at the door to catch her breath. "That was close," she said, glancing at her watch as she pulled out the seat next to his. "He isn't even coming at all today, sleepy head," he said. He had seen the punch coming but couldn't duck fast enough. "Ouch," he yelped in feigned anguish as Àshàké's fist landed on his solid left shoulder.

Kalu Ibe was handsome, rich, and funny.

The only surviving son of one of the many northern-based, Igbo millionaire merchants; he was the typical rich kid with the full accompaniments of the easy life and expensive toys. With fees at the high end of the spectrum, Johnson was host to many like Kal. But his deep pockets, his penchant for pretty girls, and, especially, his sleek garish red Mercedes Benz sports car made him stand out.

Within a year of their matriculation, he had become a regular feature at major campus parties and the crush of many girls. Although they were course mates and therefore constantly in each other's space, Àshàké was careful, almost deliberate, in keeping her distance. It had worked perfectly well the first two years. He hadn't even appeared to be aware of her existence.

A chance meeting at the social sciences building at the beginning of their third year had changed all that, however. She had been waiting alone for about an hour for the dean's secretary before he sauntered in. "Hi, Àshàké," he had greeted, his tone friendly and familiar. It would have been hard to tell he was speaking to her directly for the first time. "Hi," she said and tried to focus on the course registration form in her hand.

He wore tennis shoes, baggy three-quarter-length shorts, and a white top with some girl-demeaning expletive emblazoned on it. Àshàké wondered how anybody could be so brazenly obscene. A familiar feeling of deep resentment was rising within her as shadowy figures from her past began to stir. She disliked this guy.

"I wanted to drop this form. I understand today is the deadline," he said as he walked over to sit one seat from her on the steel row of chairs. She could smell his cologne as he walked past her. Strangely, though she had seen him practically every day on and off for months in a row; up close, he was somewhat different.

"I've been here for almost an hour, she had to attend a meeting with the dean," she said, momentarily looking up at him, trying to sound as normal as possible. He was gazing intently at her, his face transparently curious. "What?" She asked, unconsciously running her hand down the buttons of her blouse as she held his gaze. "Your hair, I never noticed it before," he said, pointing briefly at her hair. Àshàké thought the child-likeness of his curiosity amusing. "I am Fulani." She said, simply.

He started laughing.

It was a loud booming laughter and he didn't seem to be able to stop.

Àshàké was beginning to bristle. "Wait... wait... I'm sorry, okay," he said trying to catch his breath, "but you'll have to do better than that!" "Which Fulani girl bears Àshàké?" he asked. "You are Yoruba." Àshàké was impressed by the accuracy of his guess in spite of herself. "And you are Igbo," she said, emphasizing the *Igbo*, as she began to laugh with him.

"Guilty as charged," he said, raising his right hand. "But seriously," he pressed her, "you look Fulani, your hair... it's lovely." Then he did something Àshàké thought only girls did: he moved over and felt her hair, rubbing the strands between his thumb and fingers. "It's natural," he said as if he had just been proven right.

"Don't touch my hair!" Àshàké snapped, only half meaning it. He laughed. Then leaning back momentarily with his brow creased as if in deep contemplation, he said, "You are beautiful."

He wasn't flirting with her. It was his personal factual assessment. Yet, she felt an unfamiliar tingle run through her and was surprised by how relaxed she felt with him.

CHAPTER 16

Their relationship had developed smoothly and seamlessly. There were no formalities, no propositions, no announcements – every stage seemed to simply flow into the next. For Àshàké, it was like being on an exhilarating romantic roller–coaster. She enjoyed the heady freedom of letting go of what little inhibitions she had and allowing Kal's world of wealth, wine, and wild parties suck her in.

It wasn't that he ever asked her to do anything; he always assumed she would. Whether it was the sex, the hangouts with his crazy friends, or the frequent road trips; she did it all because she wanted to.

It wasn't his wealth; it was his personality.

There was something unusual, almost mysterious, about Kal's openness. Although Àshàké knew he had several girlfriends on and off campus, she didn't mind because he didn't seem to think she should. Whether it was escapades with rich girlfriends from his upscale neighborhood back home, fawning daughters of old family friends, or his present and ex-girlfriends on campus; he would talk and laugh about them without qualms.

They were an integral part of his privileged life. He was charming and generous, and although she knew he was not exclusive to her, he still managed to somehow make her feel special. Kal held no lasting promise, yet Àshàké was content to relish the here and the now.

Her second visit to Mike Kuliji's flat was the first time she ever saw Kal rattled.

Fast-talking and bearded, the young Dr. Kuliji had been deployed as a medical officer to the Johnson Medical Center under the National Youth Service Scheme about the time they resumed the first semester of their third year. He soon became an integral part of the licentious underworld of the Johnson student community and a close friend of Kal's.

Since reproductive health services were hardly available to students at the center, word had quickly gone around that Dr. Kuliji helped out 'distressed' girls in his flat at the non-academic staff quarters. The improvised operating theater, as Àshàké was later to find out, was his bathroom.

Her recurrent urinary symptoms within the first few months of her liaison with Kal plus her subsequent missed periods meant she was a frequent guest at Dr. Mike's flat. "Doc will sort you out and you'll be fine,' Kal would always say. Like with everything else, he never thought any of it a big deal.

Àshàké knew what was happening. Despite Dr. Kuliji's frequent reassurances, she always dreaded the prospect of catching something severe or untreatable.

It was Workers' Day holiday and, for some reason, Kal was unusually irritable. Àshàké had come to his place the night before but was wary of breaking the news to him - she was pregnant again. "When are you going to grow up," he had screamed when she eventually got around to telling him. "Damn, I don't know how much longer I can put up with this rubbish!" Àshàké was close to tears as he got up and stormed out of the room.

He was right, she should learn to take care of herself.

While Kal was generous in providing for her, expecting him to protect her was asking for too much. His abundant finances had more than compensated for the life her relationship with Faruk had primed her for. In retrospect, maybe the relationship itself had been an unconscious fallback – especially as the pecuniary benefits of that relationship had abruptly dried up, and with it, the gradual atrophy of the emotional connection she once felt to Faruk.

It had been six months of no communication and Faruk had become a distant memory.

Kal was quiet as he drove her to NAS Flat 14 that evening. His pleasantries with Dr. Kuliji, besides their usual fist bump, were subdued. After the usual questions about her last period and so on, Dr. Mike was ready for business.

Àshàké knew the drill. Within an hour, she would be sleeping peacefully on Dr. Mike's bed; business taken care of. She had always wondered how the diminutive doctor managed to move her unconscious five-foot-ten frame from the improvised couch on the bathtub to the large bed in his single room. That was probably why he always insisted Kal stayed around

As she shed her clothes and stepped into the bathroom, she felt the familiar heave of her stomach as the strong smell of antiseptics hit her. The continuous stream of Johnson girls meant Dr. Kuliji's "theater" had to always be set. Yet, Àshàké wondered how this small space could possibly serve this as well as the actual purpose for which it was originally designed at the same time.

Kal's coldness towards her had made her a bit edgy. She had tried to apologize but he had been quiet and distant. "Excuse me," was all he had said earlier in the day as he shunned her attempt to put her arms around him.

She trembled as her bare back touched the freshly cleaned surface of the wooden board. Taking a deep breath, she wondered whose blood was last washed off the couch. Dr. Kuliji was busy as usual sorting steel surgical instruments, hands donning gloves he had pulled out of a sterile pack in the small ceramic wash basin. Àshàké looked forward to the needle prick and the oblivion that would follow as she lost grip of consciousness. "Make a tight fist and relax," was the last thing she heard him say as he applied the rubber tourniquet just above her right elbow.

She remembered feeling the needle prick, then gradually beginning to float away. Then came the chemical rush to her head. *Something wasn't right*, she thought in her delirium. The ceiling above was moving and she was vaguely aware of sliding off the couch and hitting the bathroom floor. She could hear Kal screaming, then a loud pounding on the door. The tightness around her chest wasn't letting her breathe. *Was she dying?*

When she came around, she was still on the floor. Her whole body felt sore and her lower belly cramped. As she lifted herself off the floor with all the strength she could muster, she felt a warm trickle run down her thighs. She was bleeding. "Calm down, Kal," she could hear Dr. Kuliji through the slightly open door, "the seizures have stopped, she'll be fine." His voice was low, almost inaudible. "She won't be fine doc; she's dead and we are finished!" Kal's voice was tense and hollow, "I've got to call my dad..."

Kal was standing on the other side of the room, his right arm supporting his forehead against the wall. Dr. Kuliji was standing behind him, his right hand on his shoulder trying to calm him down. "Kal," Àshàké called out weakly. They had both swung around; eyes wide as they stared at her. She must have passed out again because she had woken up later at the University Medical Centre. "You miscarried," a nurse later informed her. "Your friends brought you here." The emphasis she had put on *friends* told Àshàké just how much she thought of them.

That Workers' Day incident had redefined their relationship. Kal had later taken her to see Dr. Umoru. He was a kindly old man with almost snow-white hair. "He and my dad have been friends for over thirty years," he had assured her. He had not told her though that the aging gynecologist had also attended at his birth over twenty years earlier. "I wonder why Kalu withheld such vital information from you," Dr. Umoru wondered aloud. Àshàké thought he made it sound as if that information was vital to her present diagnosis.

He had done some deep examination of her lower tummy, poked around her insides with his gloved fingers, and done an ultrasound scan. Though the examination had come with significant discomfort, Dr. Umoru's approach was empathetic, yet professional.

"You have something going on down there, Àshàké," he said as he meticulously slid a swab stick back into its holder. "We'll give you some antibiotics and something else to keep you out of trouble in the future," He had said the "trouble" part with a knowing conspiratorial smile.

"Am I going to be alright?" Àshàké asked, visibly anxious. "I don't see why not," he said as the nurse came in to lead her to the treatment area. "I'll be more careful in the future though if I were you."

Àshàké had spent the three-hour drive back to Johnson lost in thought. Dr. Umoru's last words kept ringing in her head. She knew she had lived recklessly, especially in the previous six months, and kept trying to shake off the haunting thought that she had probably suffered some sort of permanent damage.

From the corner of her eye, she observed Kal. He had become unusually introspective since the incident at Dr. Mike's place. His fingers rested comfortably on the small steering wheel of the Mercedes. His face was thoughtful, his body tense. "I think we need to slow down a bit," he suddenly said as he swung into the five-hundred-meter beautifully-landscaped dual carriageway that led up to the main entrance of Johnson, "Maybe we should just be friends."

He took his eyes off the road briefly to glance at her. Àshàké said nothing.

It had taken them the larger part of the semester, but they had eventually settled into a comfortable rhythm of friendship which, though less intimate, was full of fun and laughter. But now this rhythm has been disrupted by a terse note from Faruk who, within the space of two years, became her benefactor, captor, and ultimately her suitor.

Captivity

CHAPTER 17

Something was different about Faruk the evening he picked her up after her discharge from the MIR. He was unusually tender towards her and murderously angry at Uncle Aminu. "That animal is on his way to hell, *Wallahi*," he swore under his breath, seething with rage. "How is he?" Àshàké asked; more out of curiosity than pity. "He is dead," he replied, his voice cold and flat.

Something about the dismissive finality of his tone made her uneasy. She had heard stories of people being shot and dumped in the bamboo forest near the parade ground but, surely, not Uncle Aminu. He was a soldier.

Faruk had promptly handed her over to Fatima when they got home. "Make sure she eats," he instructed before leaving for the officers' mess.

As usual, she had woken up when he drove in at about midnight. That night he hadn't just peeked into her bedroom and gone on to bed as usual; he had come in.

Àshàké could make out his silhouette against the hallway light as he approached the bed. He had hesitated as he got within reach of her, turning to glance at the hallway through the open door. His attitude was furtive and unsure. The smell of his woody cologne filled her nostrils as his towering figure got closer. Above the slow whir of the ceiling fan, she could hear his heavy breathing.

He stood there looking down at her for what seemed like an eternity before leaning over to brush some hair off her face. The feel of his fingers on her forehead was rough but soothing. He hesitated, and then made to leave. "Good evening, Sir," Àshàké said. She didn't know why she did that. Maybe she wanted him to stay. "I didn't know you were awake," he said as he slowly sat on the bed.

When she woke up the next morning at the familiar sound of Fatima's housekeeping, he was gone. Àshàké touched the dent on the pillow where he had lain. His smell still hung in the room like an accusing presence. The night before had been surreal. She wondered whether Fatima had heard or seen anything. She was a very jolly woman but beneath her sweet facade, Àshàké suspected Fatima knew a lot about a lot.

"Àshàké, do you know that *Oga* likes small girls?" she had casually asked her two days later as they loaded the washing machine. "*Eeehen,*" Àshàké replied, raising a brow in mock surprise. "That is why he and Hajiya are always fighting." Fatima had said nothing else but, again, Àshàké thought she had a lot more to say.

Whatever Fatima's intention had been, her confirmation of this fault line in Faruk's marriage made Àshàké feel sorry for him, and with that came a strange desire to get even closer. Although she had never met Mrs. Faruk, she began to resent her.

In retrospect, it was all the confusing emotions of teenage crush; a situation Faruk took maximum advantage of.

Faruk groomed Àshàké with his affection and his gifts. Their intimacy wasn't so much physical as it was emotional. She soon developed a strong urge to always be with him and when he wasn't home, which was most of the day, she yearned for him - craved the attention he so lavishly showered on her.

Unaccustomed to attention, she had lapped up Faruk's skilfully deployed affection, and before long, it was all she lived for. Faruk wanted to be abreast of every detail of her life. He would call from work to ask about what she watched on TV, what she ate, what she was wearing... Soon he began to buy her clothes and underwear and would typically tell her what he wanted her to be wearing when he got home.

Fatima was displeased.

Àshàké could tell from her fussiness. She had become irritable and touchy about everything Àshàké said or did. Whatever she had seen or heard the day Faruk slept in her room disrupted the developing bond of affection between them. She missed Fatima's jokes and her childhood stories about growing up in her hometown and playing *suwe* with other kids in her community.

Àshàké could not get the hang of the game although Fatima had tried several times to teach her how to hop between the multiple boxes she drew on the ground and throw the pebbles. She found watching *Papa Ajasco* and *Fuji House of Commotion* on TV a lot more fun.

Her days became long and very lonely. She wished Fatima would say something; anything. But instead, she would just go about her chores in studied silence - not speaking to her, except to take her request at meal times.

"Àshàké, do you know that you and Jamila are both sixteen?" Fatima asked one morning as Àshàké stood in front of the hallway mirror struggling to get into a tight-fitting black dress Faruk had bought for her the day before. Àshàké's heart skipped. Fatima's voice sounded accusatory and, coming after almost a whole week of the silent treatment, she was caught off-guard.

"This is not Jamila's dress *o*," Àshàké said, defensively. "Who said anything about a dress," Fatima said as she abruptly walked off muttering something to herself about parents and poor home training. The disdain in her attitude had made Àshàké feel like a piece of dirt. She had abandoned the dress on the hallway floor and spent the rest of the day in bed.

Despite her muddled-up emotions, Àshàké knew enough to understand that what was happening between herself and Faruk was wrong. That didn't stop her from feeling hopelessly entangled; almost obsessed. With the benefit of hindsight, she imagined that he too must have had his sober moments… like the night she slept in his room in Jamila's nightgown. He had seemed visibly upset when he stepped out of the shower and saw her curled up in bed, wearing the pink sleeping dress.

"No. No…, y-you shouldn't be wearing t-that," he stuttered, his right hand involuntarily flying to his face as if to ward off the sight of her. "That belongs to my daughter." He had sounded really distraught as he turned away.

That night he was withdrawn and a bit restless. Although he had warmed up again to her by the next day, the message of that incident was not lost on her.

She could have been his daughter, and Faruk knew it.

CHAPTER 18

Faruk never entered her room again after that first night. But then, she was hardly in bed when he got home - she always stayed up to wait for him. Àshàké always looked forward to sitting on the rug in the elegant sitting room and talking with him while they prepared for bed.

Hajiya Jumai called every night; usually at the same time - just before midnight. He never took her calls in Àshàké's presence and she would strain to piece together their conversation from his usually harsh but lowered voice. "Jumai, I am not going to let you run my life, *kaji ko?*" she overheard him say one Monday night. He had seemed particularly upset and whatever she was saying at the other end wasn't helping matters.

"I repeat, Fati is my employee and she has no right to talk to you about me. *Wallahi,* it is insulting." His voice was high-pitched and strained. He didn't seem to care if she heard.

"Why do you two always fight?" Àshàké asked him when he finally returned to the living room minutes later. She had snuggled close to him as he sat on the rug in hopes of providing some comfort. "Go to bed, please," he growled. She tried to protest but he never said another word and she gave up and went to bed. As she struggled to go to sleep, she could hear him pacing around the hallway, then voices. Someone was crying. *Aunty Fati?*

The next morning was unusual.

An air of stillness hung heavily in the house. She hadn't woken up to the familiar sound of Fatima's housekeeping or her loud singing. It was 7.45 am from Jamila's bedside clock. Faruk would be at the office already.

She got off the bed and walked barefooted to the door. The solid wooden door had no bolts and she had never seen the key to the lock. Although Àshàké could easily have kept it shut, she always went to bed with the door slightly ajar because that was what Faruk wanted. She could easily have heard Fatima if she was anywhere in the house.

Although they had spoken very little in recent days, she always sought her out once she woke up to say Good Morning. "Aunty Fati!" she called out as she simultaneously strained her ears for any familiar sounds. Silence.

It took her only a few minutes to realize Fatima wasn't in the house. Her door just around the corner from the kitchen balcony was shut with a bunch of keys hanging from the lock outside. When she turned the steel knob and peeped into the room, it was orderly but deserted. The only sign that Fatima ever lived there was the black slippers with the multi-colored edges she always wore for her chores. She had left them, placed neatly side by side, just by the door.

Àshàké remembered how she would mercilessly tease her about her "see-through" slippers because of the holes her heels had created in them.

There was a rustling sound in the kitchen. *Aunty Fati is back*, she thought. As she stepped back into the balcony, she saw Faruk, multiple white polythene bags in hand, standing by the kitchen door. She hadn't heard the car. The smell of fried Chicken told her where he had been.

"She is gone," he said as if reading her mind. "Gone? Where?" She asked, suppressing an unfamiliar feeling of panic. For some reason, she suddenly didn't feel safe with him. "We've not seen each other this morning, have we?" He said, raising a disapproving brow. "S-sorry. Good morning.... Sir," she said, taking the white bags and side-stepping him to drop them on the kitchen table.

"I wasn't sure whether you could cook so I decided to go to Betty's Spices before going to the office." He was trying hard to sound normal, almost jovial, but À̀shàké knew something was wrong.

"Where is Aunty Fati? Why did she leave?" À̀shàké asked as he put his arms around her slim waist and tried to hold her against the kitchen table. But instead of snuggling up to him as she normally would, she pushed her arms between them, both palms firmly on his chest. But her efforts were futile as he held firmly to the table on both sides of her, effortlessly pinning her against it. "She wanted me to send you away... and I wasn't going to do that," he said, trying to restrain and placate her all at once.

It suddenly all made sense. The heated exchange with his wife, the sound of sobbing last night; that was Aunty Fati and it had all been about her. She pulled violently away from him and ran out of the kitchen. She was overwhelmed with guilt.

À̀shàké knew Fatima had no living parents or close relatives. She had nowhere to go.

Faruk and his troops had picked her up with a deep machete cut to the back of her neck after some marauders burnt down her farming village in Kadima during a midnight raid. When the troops arrived almost two hours later, they found her naked and unconscious amongst charred human remains and burnt mud huts.

À̀shàké had wept the night Faruk narrated the story to her. Fatima never told anyone what she saw or how she managed to escape the fire. À̀shàké always remembered how she would often rub the fleshy scar at the back of her neck and say, "*Oga* Faruk is my savior."

Now, where was she going to go?

She was throwing her things into a large polythene bag that served as an improvised laundry bag when he came into the room. "What do you think you are doing?" His voice had a cold edginess to it. By now she was crying profusely. "I want to go home," she said. "Young lady, you have no home; this is where you belong now," he said, his irritation laced with sarcasm.

He threw the bags of food on the bed and walked out, shutting the door behind him. À̀shàké heard a key turn in the lock.

It had seemed like a whole day but it was only about four hours later that she heard his car in the driveway. He was speaking in low tones with someone – a woman. *Had he changed his mind and decided to bring back Aunty Fati?* She heard the key turn in the lock again. "Guess who's here," he said, almost cheerfully as he opened the door ushering her into the narrow hallway, towards the sitting room.

She tried to restrain her legs from running. Aunty Fati was back and everything was going to be alright again. She was going to tell her how sorry she was for all that had happened.

Then she froze.

Sitting in the padded armchair across from her was Aunty Iyabo. Although her face was partially concealed by a dark veil, Àshàké could see how gaunt she looked and the odd appearance of her face. Her right eyelid was drooping and the left side of her mouth was curved slightly upwards. "Ash-a-k…" she tried to call her name but her speech was slurred and the effort to speak distorted her face even more. Àshàké could see her trying unsuccessfully to stop a drop of spittle dripping from the side of her mouth. "W-w-welcome, Aunty," Àshàké said, hands by her sides; tightly gripping the sides of her dress to keep them steady.

"The doctors said she suffered a stroke and a fractured skull from the fall," Faruk said from behind her. For the first time since the incident, Àshàké felt responsible and truly sorry for hurting her so badly. She crossed the room and sat on the arm of the chair and hugged her tightly. Only Aunty Iyabo's left arm moved.

"I'm so sorry, Aunty. I will come and look after you…" Her tears were flowing freely by now. "CO has asked them to transfer her to the army referral hospital in Kali for rehabilitation", Faruk said, "Bidemi is joining her father's family in Lagos."

Àshàké didn't know what all of that meant for her but she knew she wanted to stay with her Aunty and help her heal. "I will stay with Aunty…" It was the firm pressure of Aunty Iyabo's hand on her thigh that stopped her. Àshàké could see her distorted mouth moving as she struggled to form the words in response to her quizzical look. It was Faruk that answered her question.

"CO has directed that you return to school and prepare for the Senior

School Certificate exams this August." His voice was impersonal and officious. Aunty Iyabo's eyes urged her.

An elderly relative was arranged to come and assist during the long hospital stay at Kali which, Àshàké was informed, the regiment would pay for. She now officially had one home and she shared it with Faruk. Strangely, Fatima's departure had disrupted their connection and drastically changed her feelings of attachment toward him. The all-consuming puppy love she felt for him had, overnight, dramatically changed into a quiet dread.

She hoped Aunty Iyabo would be home in about four months when she should be done with her exams so she could return home. Yet the prospect of spending four whole months alone with him in the house troubled her.

But she need not have bothered.

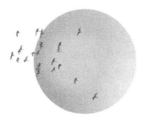

CHAPTER 19

It had taken approximately three days for her to be re-enrolled at the Command Secondary School. Although she had left in the second term of her fifth form, it only took a phone call from the CO for the principal to get her enrolled in the sixth form. She had resolved to do her best to make good grades even though she was not sure what value that would have in her uncertain future.

Faruk ensured she got everything she needed and more. "Focus on your books and make me proud," he told her on her first official day at school. "Silas will take you to and from school." Àshàké had wished she could walk to school like she and Bidemi usually did, but most of the children from the officers' quarters were chauffeured to school by the batsmen.

Faruk had left the keys to her room for her after Aunty Iyabo's visit and she had begun to lock her door whenever she went to bed. But he never opened it or looked in on her again whenever he got home from the officers' mess. She noticed he would just say hello, and ask if she needed anything, but not much else. She could tell something was weighing heavily on his mind but felt strangely indifferent.

Silas, the new batsman, was soft-spoken and very smart. He had told her he was an English graduate from City University and had joined the army with the hope that he would eventually get the opportunity to attend the academy. Àshàké usually enjoyed the way he mimicked the CO and Faruk.

"Those guys speak terrible English," he would say. "The day they will catch you *eehn*," À̀shàké would warn him as they both burst into laughter. He was only twenty-three and À̀shàké had connected with him in a way she never did with Faruk.

After Fatima's departure, Faruk, using his influence as regimental adjutant, had transferred Silas from the officers' mess where, as head chef, the young soldier's culinary skills had become sort of legendary. The other officers had kicked against it but he had courted the CO and eventually gotten his way. This meant that apart from his regular duties as batsman, Silas also spent a lot of time around the house helping out with cooking and sundry domestic chores.

But beyond filling the void created by Fatima's departure; he also provided the male affection Faruk had masterfully groomed À̀shàké to constantly crave. He would do most of the chores while she was still at school so that they would spend long hours together after he brought her home.

With Silas, she was introduced to an entirely new vista of feminine expression. Their relationship was both fun and physically intense but, unlike with Captain Faruk, she felt like they both owned it. "One day, *Oga* is going to find out and I'll be dead," he said one evening as he ran his fingers through her wavy hair; a hint of trepidation in his voice. À̀shàké had raised her head from his chest to look at his face. His eyes were distant and reflective. "But I'm not his wife, can't I have a boyfriend?" she queried petulantly. "You won't understand, À̀shàké... you won't," he said, as he gently pushed her off him and slowly got dressed.

His words had unsettled her but little did either of them know how close doomsday was for him.

Everyone in the barrack community was familiar with Faruk's reputation for ruthlessness. Rumor even had it that during a brief stint with the ECOMOG forces in Sierra Leone, he had fatally shot a senior officer during a row over a call girl. It had taken his extensive family connections within the top echelons of the military to save him from a court martial. À̀shàké had had a sense of foreboding but she was too entangled with Silas to care.

It was a Monday, exactly two months after she started school. Silas arrived at the school earlier than usual and seemed quite excited. Àshàké thought she recognized the mood. "Let me guess; salaries have been paid!" She teased, searching his face as she settled into the car. "She has come!" he exclaimed, clapping his hands loudly together as if a key prediction of his just came to pass. "Who has come? She asked, already amused. "Hajiya. *Oga*'s wife!" Àshàké's bladder suddenly felt full. "N–no, it can't be…" She was trying to think. "*Oga* doesn't even know yet," he announced, almost gleefully.

"I can't go back there," she said finally, almost to herself. "Of course, you can!" He said, "Actually, she asked me to come and get you." Àshàké was in full panic now. "I need to pee," she said abruptly. "Be my guest," Silas said as he pulled the car off the hilly road that led to the married officers' quarters. For some reason, he seemed to be thoroughly enjoying himself.

She braced herself as they pulled into the driveway to the house.

Hajiya Jumai was a small dark woman with bright intelligent eyes. Her prominent aquiline nose reminded Àshàké of a fairy witch from a movie she had recently seen. "You are Àshàké," she said as Àshàké timidly stepped out of the car. Her voice was husky and authoritative. Àshàké cringed. "My-my Aunty fell and CO s-said…" she began to explain but Mrs. Faruk's raised hand cut her short. "Enough! I know," she said, "It's not your fault." Her tone was neutral. There was no accusation; no anger.

 "Silas, let me see *Oga* CO," she said as she picked up her handbag and walked briskly to the car. It was as if she had wanted to visually evaluate her before deciding on her next line of action. The look Silas gave her as they drove off seemed to tell her to prepare for war.

Silas did not return to the house that day.

Àshàké had expected him to call her to let her know what was going on, but after three hours of pacing, she couldn't take it anymore. When she dialed his number and didn't get a response, she decided to leave him a message to call her back. About an hour later he sent her a short message instead:

Àshàké, it's not looking good.

They are at each other's throats in the CO's office.

Hajiya is likely to throw you out tonight.

You can move to my place.

The text message proved to be a costly mistake.

Àshàké had immediately packed her bags and braced herself for the inevitable. She didn't want Mrs. Faruk to meet her in Jamila's room or anywhere within the house. With her scanty personal belongings hurriedly stuffed into her school bag, she sat out on the portable camp bed Faruk usually set up under the sturdy *frangipani* tree by the external carport on hot days. Quietly she sobbed.

Faruk was right; she had no home to go back to.

She hadn't had a bite after breakfast yet she felt no desire for food. Her entire being felt like one tightly knotted bundle of nerves.

Faruk was drunk when he returned home sometime after midnight.

He rarely was, yet she could tell from his talkativeness. She felt all men were that way when they were drunk. She imagined that was why Uncle Aminu talked so much.

He sat inside the car for a while; the full headlights on Àshàké's huddled figure. When the lights went out and she finally heard the car door slam, she hugged her bag tightly to her chest squinting as she tried to readjust to the semi-darkness.

"So, you were going to move in with your new boyfriend, *ba*?" His voice was heavy with contempt. "*Shege, dan iska!* The bastard!" he cursed. "That boy insulted me, *wallahi.*" Àshàké cowered. "He sent the text but…" she tried to explain. "Shut up, you cheap little prostitute!" He was almost screaming. "That randy bastard will pay, I assure you…" The meanness in his tone sounded familiar. Where was Silas? She felt a cold chill creep over her.

She didn't want anything to happen to Silas. Remembering how pensive he had been the last night they were together, she wished she had taken his concerns a bit more seriously.

"One day, *Oga* is going to find out and I'll be dead," she recalled him saying. But how could Faruk; Silas was so harmless.

He was just about a meter from her, a towering figure pacing menacingly; passing his keys from one hand to the other. Àshàké could imagine his teeth were clenched and his lips pressed thinly together – the way they were whenever something ticked him off. He seemed to be trying to decide what to do with her. There was no sign of Hajiya Jumai.

Àshàké waited with bated breath. She felt like a cornered prey as she followed his every move with her eyes.

"Get in the house," he said quietly.

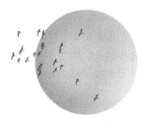

CHAPTER 20

Àshàké always enjoyed the warmth of Faruk's embrace with its odd mix of fatherly affection and romantic tenderness. But that night was different. There had been no words; just domineering mastery as he vented his anger and frustration on her young body. She had woken up on the sitting room couch where she had eventually cried herself to sleep. Her lips felt swollen and she ached all over from his long night of drunken brutality.

When he ordered her back into the house the night before, it had crossed her mind for a fleeting moment that he would kill her. The subsequent events had been surreal; Faruk tearing at her clothes, squeezing her throat... She had felt like a bystander; mentally dissociating herself from the experience.

When she woke up in the morning, her school bag was just by the entrance but its contents were spread out on the table. He must have been going through them. She reached for her torn school uniform and tried to cover her nakedness.

When he emerged moments later from the hallway, the pink phone he had bought her just before she started school was in his hand. "You whore, so, after all I did for you..." he said, tossing the phone at her. The lighted screen confirmed her worst fears; he had been reading her chats with Silas!

From the corner of her eyes, she saw him walk over to the fridge and pick out a bottle of water. The intensity of his rage as he violently unscrewed the cap and began to drink made her cringe. She watched in wide-eyed fear as his beaky Adam's apple bobbed up and down as he impatiently downed the water. His normally clean-shaven face had grown a stubble of beard and Àshàké noticed several wisps of grey. He looked older.

"My wife left because she couldn't accept you." His voice was momentarily sad. I'm sorry was all she wanted to say but didn't. It had been all her fault, yet she felt trapped and unsure of what to do. In just a few weeks she had brought so much sorrow to so many people. She thought of Jamila and Bala; like Bidemi, she knew they would never forgive her. And now, Aunty Fati was homeless.

"I've made up my mind." His voice interrupted her thoughts. Holding the dress close to her body, she turned to look at him over the back of the couch. *What was it this time?* He was standing by the hallway door. "You will stay here and continue school," he said. It was his decision. As he often did in the months that followed, he gave her no options; no say.

After he left for Saturday morning sports, Àshàké had gathered her scattered belongings to settle back into the room she had once daydreamed she would someday share with Jamila.

Now, that was never going to be.

She had found the reality of her situation ironic. Jamila was most probably never going to come and now, in a sense, she owned the room. As she made to put away her clothes, her eyes fell on the framed photograph hanging above the chest of drawers and Jamila's pretty face smiling down at her. She had promptly unhooked it from the wall and placed it face-down on the bedside drawer. The room suddenly felt haunted by the presence of this pretty girl she was now never going to meet.

The house was soon to get a second ghost: Gundu, the taciturn batsman Faruk got as a replacement for Silas. Something about his dour face and drooping eyes had unsettled Àshàké from the first day he resumed duties. And the way he would follow her with his eyes whenever he was in the house, which was almost always, made her skin crawl.

For some reason, he was always there before she left for school and never left until she got back. Àshàké had thought she could extract some information on Silas' whereabouts from the dull-looking soldier and subsequently made some half-hearted effort to be friendly.

"*Forget Salas*," he said with a scowl the only day she attempted to prod him. Something about the way he said it quashed the last vestige of hope she had of ever seeing Silas again. Yet she longed to know what happened – whatever it was.

Although they hardly spoke, Gundu's very presence around the house bothered her. She found his constant teeth-picking disgusting and the shrill sound of his small radio irritating. But the afternoon she came out of the bathroom to find him in her bedroom was the last straw.

She was reaching for her body lotion when she observed the shadowy figure in the dressing mirror. She swung around, her heart racing, only to see Gundu advancing toward her. Memories of that August afternoon encounter with Uncle Aminu two years earlier had come rushing back.

"*I want to tell you am going*," he said as he stopped within reach of her. He had a toothpick in his mouth as always and Àshàké could smell his sweaty body. "H-h-how did you get in here?" She had meant to scream, but her voice was barely above a whisper. She was trembling uncontrollably as she held the small towel firmly around her wet body. "*I use ma key*," he answered, holding up a bunch of keys.

His face was expressionless. '*We see tomorrow*," he said as he stared at her for a few more seconds before slowly and noiselessly backing out of the room – all the while never taking his eyes off her.

Àshàké had sobbed uncontrollably. How many times had he entered her room in her absence? She shuddered as she thought of the many hot afternoons when she would take a nap barely dressed in the assumed privacy of her room. How could Faruk give Gundu a spare key to her bedroom?

It was way past midnight before Faruk got home from the mess. The incident with Gundu had left her shaken and she was too scared even to leave the room. His loud whistling as he entered the house told her what to expect and she inwardly braced herself. The stifling smell of beer and tobacco; and his loveless passion had become part of her existence but the encounter with Gundu that afternoon had stirred something else in her that was almost forgotten - defiance.

"Gundu was in this room," she said as he made to release the spaghetti straps of her nightie – he had ordered her to always have one on when he got home. As usual, he had barely looked at her; and if he heard her, he showed no sign. She tried again as she stepped out of the thin silk dress which now lay around her ankles on the floor, "I was bathing and he unlocked the door and came in," she said. He stopped momentarily. Àshàké could see his face in the dim light. He looked bored and slightly irritated. It was that same "not again..." look he would have whenever Hajiya's call came in.

"Gundu was doing his job, okay?" he said finally, a hint of controlled impatience in his authoritative tone. "But this is Jamila's room, h-he can't just come in here!" She said, near exasperated.

The mention of his daughter's name did something to him. He recoiled from her as if he had been stung and gently sank to the floor; knees drawn up to his chest, as he placed both hands on his forehead. "I can't do this anymore," he muttered, "*Wallahi*, I can't." Although Àshàké could not imagine it, she thought he was sobbing as she watched his shoulders heave again and again. But despite his apparent despondency, Àshàké was indifferent: she just sat on the bed and waited for him.

He never came.

"Get dressed, please," he said a few minutes later as he rose and quietly left the room, shutting the door behind him. He was gone by the time she woke up the next morning. It was a Saturday and he would normally wait around for Gundu to report for duty. She hadn't quite known what to expect and was glad she didn't have to face him so soon after the incident of the night before.

The Road to Johnson

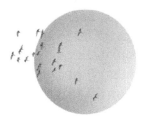

CHAPTER 21

Àshàké's journey to Johnson was as dramatic as it was unexpected. Her relationship with Faruk had worsened after the incident with Gundu and, although he still ran her life - mostly through Gundu who snooped on her around the community and was practically in her every space at home, he seemed to have been permanently put off any sort of sexual intimacy with her.

This served to free her up mentally to focus on the last few months of school. A decent High School Certificate result was her reward. Faruk had seemed indifferent to her success in the exams and, although she was not surprised, it still hurt. Being the closest thing to a functional family she had, she had expected him to share in her joy.

Six months after her final exams, Àshàké's place in Faruk's life and home had become even fuzzier. He remained distant yet fiercely possessive. She was a precocious seventeen-year-old with exceptional good looks and Faruk was aware that not a few of his brother officers had their eyes on her.

"The day you let Abdul touch you, you are finished!" he had growled at her one afternoon after he got back from a squash game and found her sitting under the *frangipani* tree with Lieutenant Abdul, the next-door neighbor from flat 6 with whom she had become good friends. Faruk had gripped her arm so tightly as he dragged her into the house that her arm had hurt for days.

As the weeks rolled into months, her frustration grew, so, she decided to confront him. "What do you and CO want from me?" She asked him pointedly one morning. "CO has been posted out," was his curt reply. The news took Àshàké by surprise. "S-so what happens to me now?" she asked - half speaking to herself. CO's redeployment meant that her fate was completely in Faruk's hands. "I'll decide when I'm ready," he said with a hint of a sneer as he picked up his keys and headed for the door.

His decision was to come faster than she had expected.

It was Friday and Faruk was home early which Àshàké thought was unusual. She had seen the tickets on the table the day before so she knew it was *Tombola* night when the mess played host to officers from other uniformed services. Faruk never took her to the *tombola*, or even to the mess for that matter – he seemed satisfied restricting her exposure to his own domestic version of vice.

Lieutenant Abdul, however, always satisfied her curiosity with graphic details of the gambling and debauchery that went on there. "What about their wives?" Àshàké once asked. "There's no marriage in the mess," he had replied, giving Àshàké a look she could not fathom.

So, this afternoon when Àshàké saw Faruk walk in and noticed Gundu in tow, she wondered what was afoot. He had barely acknowledged her presence as they headed straight to the seldom-used guest bedroom and began to clean it out. Aunty Fati always kept it meticulously clean before her unceremonious departure and the room had remained locked ever since.

Àshàké knew Gundu could easily have handled this task and wondered why Faruk had to be personally involved. "My sister is arriving this evening," he informed her as he heaved a broken settee through the living room to the garage. Àshàké hadn't been quite sure she heard right. "Your sister?" Her hands were already clammy. "Yes, Hajiya Meiro, she'll be staying the weekend." Àshàké's mind was in full overdrive by now. She sensed that her life was, once again, about to be disrupted.

Hajiya Meiro was Faruk's older sister and only sibling. She was a widow who had amassed tremendous wealth importing and distributing Arabian fabrics and jewelry. Almost ten years older than Faruk, Àshàké knew she had seen Faruk through high school after their parent's death. Her extensive contacts within the military establishment had also secured Faruk a place at the academy and she had remained the dominant influence in her younger brother's life.

According to Aunty Fati, the only time he ever went against her express wishes was when he insisted on marrying Hajiya Jumai, hinting that her overbearing influence and Faruk's unquestioning loyalty were partly responsible for the constant turbulence in their marriage.

It was an unusual evening of preparations. Faruk ordered new bed sheets and a clean set of duvets. Some soldiers from the workshop came in to look at the electrical fittings and check on the plumbing. Faruk had meticulously checked and rechecked everything. Àshàké thought his fussiness had a hint of anxiety. She also noticed that he warmed up to her; somewhat.

With everyone occupied with one task or the other, she had decided to busy herself with cleaning the kitchen; a task that had fallen to the batsmen since Fatima left.

"Thank you..." It was Faruk. He was leaning against the kitchen door, shirtless, a towel rag in his hand. "I miss you around the house," he said as he wiped his brow with the back of his hand. "B-but I'm..." His sentiment had thrown her off balance yet she tried to remind him of the obvious. *But I'm here*, she thought to herself instead as she dropped her gaze and went back to her task.

"Hajiya is looking forward to meeting you," he said quietly. Àshàké looked up at him, unable to hide her surprise. "Does she know me?" She asked, her voice slightly raised in alarm. "I told her," he said, sounding uncharacteristically unsure as he quietly walked away.

It was almost 7 pm when Hajiya Meiro eventually arrived from the airport in a Toyota Hilux truck. Faruk had detailed one of the pool drivers to stand by and pick her up whenever she arrived. Àshàké watched her alight from the vehicle through the window of her room.

She was a tall chubby woman with a distinct air of affluence. Her facial resemblance to her younger brother was striking but her glowing delicate skin, unlike Faruk's, spoke of a life spent mostly indoors.

The events of the rest of that evening were both fast-paced and full of drama.

"Where is my *Amariya*?" Àshàké could hear her ask as she approached the front door. *Wife? Who was she talking about?* she wondered. "*Wallahi*, I've been looking forward to meeting our new wife." Àshàké was now standing in the hallway and could see her clearly while adjusting her dress in front of the mirror; inwardly bracing herself for their impending encounter. "Hajiya, I told you it is not like that..." Faruk was protesting meekly.

Àshàké was wearing a flowing caftan Faruk had bought her almost six months before. She was grateful she had draped the dark silk veil she found in Jamila's room on her hair. It gave her a strange sense of belonging.

"*Sanu do zua*, welcome" Àshàké greeted her in faultless Hausa as she entered the sitting room. "Wow, she is so pretty," Hajiya's face was suddenly alight as she threw her arms wide open. The invitation was unmistakable. Àshàké hesitated, then half-heartedly walked into her open arms. Her floral aroma enveloped her as she smothered her in her embrace. There was something about the lavish affection of this strange woman that made Àshàké uneasy but she was to find out soon enough.

Letting Àshàké go after what felt like forever, she looked her over and announced, matter-of-factly, "*Wallahi*, my brother will marry you!" She was a woman not given to preambles; she demanded what she wanted - and usually got it. From the corner of her eye, Àshàké could see Faruk helplessly flop down onto the couch. "Hajiya, she is just seventeen and still has school," he protested.

"That witch Jumai was sixteen, have you forgotten?" Àshàké cringed at the icy viciousness in her voice as she mouthed Mrs. Faruk's name. But, in a split second, she was all sweetness again. "I will send you to Johnson, my dear, and you will make me very proud."

Within fifteen minutes of her arrival, and meeting Àshàké; even before she took a seat, Hajiya Meiro had decided Àshàké's fate. As had become the rule with all that had to do with Faruk, nobody asked Àshàké what she thought.

And so began her journey to the prestigious Idris Johnson Abubakar University.

Although her performance in the matriculation examinations was less than stellar, Hajiya had no problems securing her a place in the Mass Communications Department at Johnson. Faruk had appeared to balk at the idea initially but in the three days, when Hajiya Meiro's presence filled the house, he had warmed up to the idea, and even more to Àshàké. Hajiya had seen to that.

For Àshàké it had felt like a weekend of multiple X-rays with Hajiya probing every aspect of her life, from her parenting to her present; from her faith to her sexuality. Although she was pleasant about it and would interject with an empathetic *"Eiyaa,"* to aspects she thought particularly poignant; she nonetheless neither accepted no nor silence for an answer.

Àshàké managed to sell her a story of sexual innocence - or so it seemed. If she didn't believe her but had merely played along, it must be because it served her immediate purpose.

"Gambo, take very good care of *Amariya*," was Hajiya Meiro's final instruction to Faruk as they helped her check in her luggage at the airport and it was one Faruk took a bit too seriously.

Àshàké was pregnant a month before she was due to leave for Johnson.

"Hajiya will not like this," Faruk muttered, the day she showed him the paper strip he had given her to pee on. "She expects me to take you to school in three weeks, not to the antenatal clinic." Eventually, he had opted to take her to see a civilian doctor friend of his for what was to be the first of many pregnancy terminations.

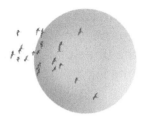

CHAPTER 22

Johnson opened a completely new vista of life for Àshàké. While she found the academics tasking, this community of mostly privileged young people with their lavish lifestyles satisfied a silent longing she always had, even in the dire poverty of Aunty Iyabo's house. Hajiya's doting benevolence provided everything she needed and more.

Between a well-funded bank account and a wardrobe frequently furnished with smart clothes, Àshàké could easily have passed for one of the many children of multi-millionaire businessmen who came to Johnson from all over the country.

The prospect of their impending marriage brought out a tenderness in Faruk that was devoid of the military rough edges to which Àshàké had become accustomed. And although he knew Hajiya provided for her needs, he still made sure he sent her a monthly allowance.

"But Hajiya already gives me more than enough," she once protested. "Hey, you are my *Amariya* not hers," he had countered in what she had come to know as his Adjutant's voice.

Although Àshàké commanded significant male attention on Campus, Faruk's frequent visits to either take her on Friday outings or to spend whole weekends together had kept even the most ambitious of her male admirers at bay. And with the army base just an hour away from campus, everyone joked that getting too close was to risk getting shot.

The first semester of Àshàké's third year marked a turning point.

"I'm now Major Umar Gambo Faruk," he announced that Friday evening as he arrived to pick her up for their usual outing. Àshàké noticed he was somewhat subdued. "Wow, congratulations!" she said, a bit concerned at his tone. "But that's supposed to be a good thing…. I mean the promotion, right?" she probed, searching his face.

He had pulled her close and buried his face in her hair. "I'm going to Kaura this week," he said. Àshàké had frozen and then pulled away to look at him again.

The Infantry Training School in Kaura was situated on the border with neighboring Niger in the arid northeast of the country. "I'm going as Second–in–Command to the Commanding Officer," he said as if trying to find something to be happy about. "Do you have to go?" Àshàké asked, feeling strangely uneasy. His response was a tolerant smile.

They had spent most of that evening without saying much to each other. Àshàké was afraid she would cry and knew that might upset him more. He, on his part, was lost in his thoughts much of the time. When he eventually dropped her off in front of her hostel, 'I'll miss you,' was all he could say as he tried to hold her one more time. She had turned away before he could see her tears and walked back to her room.

It turned out to be their last goodbye.

Àshàké had looked forward to hearing from him but a full month later, he hadn't called nor gotten in touch. Her efforts at reaching Hajiya Meiro for information were futile and she had concluded she was most probably globetrotting as usual. Several fruitless efforts later, she was close to becoming frantic. But after six long months, things had become quite nice and cozy with Kal and she had all but moved on.

Now Gundu's unexpected visit the evening before was threatening to send her world into another tailspin. She could recognize Faruk's handwriting although the words were uncharacteristically poorly spaced.

I have not been feeling well. Faruk.

'How did you get this?" she had asked Gundu after she read the terse note written on a sheet of army letterhead paper. He was already on his way back to the army truck and had turned around only briefly to look at her. There was a deep sadness in his eyes as he stepped back into the truck; still not speaking a word. What else did he know? Àshàké wondered.

As he made a tight U-turn and drove off, Àshàké stood there staring down at the note and then at the truck as it disappeared in the distance. Her subsequent frantic calls to Hajiya still didn't get through. The look on Gundu's face deeply troubled her.

Surely, if Faruk was ill, the Army had enough treatment facilities to look after him. But deep down, she knew; *something wasn't right.*

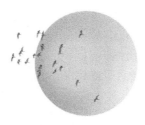

CHAPTER 23

"Babe are you okay?" It hadn't taken Kal long to notice that something was wrong as they bantered in class that morning. Àshàké had no plans of discussing Faruk's note or even mentioning his illness. That relationship just wasn't something she and Kal talked about. Although her *military connection* was common knowledge amongst their friends, there seemed to be a tacit agreement between them never to bring up Faruk – and they never did.

Kal was that way about anything that could potentially bother him and that suited Àshàké just fine in this instance. "I'm fine," she said guardedly and they had left it at that. But before nightfall that day, they were to confront Faruk and the fallouts of that relationship.

It was about 4.30pm when Àshàké's phone rang. "You don't know me, but I know you with *Oga* Faruk," the heavily accented female voice at the other end said. Àshàké assumed it was one of the many officers' wives whom Faruk oversaw as adjutant. The regiment, through his office, would usually attend to their pressing welfare needs as the army's way of ensuring their husbands stayed focused while on deployment.

With most of the men deployed to foreign missions, their wives spent the ample time they had on their hands fuelling the barrack gossip mill and engaging in sundry mischiefs. The mention of Faruk's name had gotten her heart racing.

"*Good evening*, Madam," she greeted; then asked, "is *Oga* Faruk okay?" There was a long pause and some muffled conversation in the background. Then finally she said, "My sister, go and test yourself, *Oga* Faruk is dead." The phone went dead before she had time to process what she had heard.

While the news of Faruk's death hit her hard, it was what she said first that filled her mind, overshadowing her grief and sending her into a panic. *Go and test yourself*. What was she talking about?

There had been a spate of deaths, purportedly from HIV/AIDS, amongst returnees from recent military missions and Àshàké was worried that Faruk may have caught it during his short but stormy deployment to ECOMOG. She also knew that no soldier who served abroad was ever believed to have died of natural causes – the grapevine and the likes of her anonymous caller saw to that. But if the insinuation about Faruk was true, she had to let Kal know.

Àshàké had no illusions that Kal had any real affection for her beyond the unbridled lust that dominated their recent dalliance, but the thoughtless self-centeredness of his outburst when she told him about Faruk had surprised, and deeply hurt her.

He was engrossed in a football game on TV when she arrived at his apartment. Ordinarily, as is usual at such times, he would hardly have heard a word she spoke. But when she said, "Faruk is dead," he slowly laid the remote control on the table as if it would detonate. Without turning his head, he asked, "what happened?" Àshàké noticed his hands were unsteady.

"I don't know, someone called and said I should get tested," she said, trying to sound as casual as possible. Kal was staring at her by now, mouth agape. Despite the chill of the air–conditioner, his face and bare muscular arms suddenly glistened with tiny beads of sweat.

"What kind of idiot are you, *eehn*?" His voice trembled and his lips quivered. Àshàké would have been amused at his undisguised melt-down if the situation were not so serious. "I'm an only son for goodness' sake, what will happen to my mother now?" he was almost whimpering. Àshàké was scared, but to see him fall apart like that disgusted her.

Yet, she tried to be reassuring; "But we don't even know what it is."

That was when he lost it. In a single flash of motion, he had grabbed her by her thick hair, his sweaty face against hers and his knuckles digging into her scalp, "you dumb, good–for–nothing whore…" Àshàké could feel his spittle spray her face as he fumed.

"Kal, please, p-please you are h-hurting me," she begged him as she frantically tried to prise his fingers from her hair. That seemed to incense him even the more. "If something happens to me, I swear…" He had left the threat hanging ominously in the air as he violently flung her onto the couch. She had fled the room feeling embarrassed and thoroughly humiliated.

The short walk to her hall of residence felt like a mile. Thoughts of the endless series of tragedies that had dogged her young life completely overwhelmed her. If this was a curse, she thought, it was a really tenacious one and there didn't seem to be any escape. She was alone, helpless, and homeless.

A familiar sign in the distance said, *Water Projects*.

She thought of making a detour onto the short winding road to the Johnson Water Storage Dam. She and Kal, on one of their many escapades, had spent hours in the shade of the short oil palm trees that dotted the vicinity of the dam. She had thoroughly enjoyed the feel of the mist brought in by the wind as it occasionally wafted across the artificial waterfall and the sound of the water as it crashed into the frothing pool in the ravine fifty meters below to continue its serpentine journey into the thick forest.

Now she could only picture her lifeless body plunging down the artificial waterfall and floating downstream in the boisterous currents – away from the abuse, the deaths, and the broken dreams. The cold comfort of death beckoned, but she demurred.

That night she hardly slept. She wished she could have gone to the health center immediately to get the tests done. At least, that way, she would know for sure – one way or another. But that would have to wait till the morning as the clinic only attended to emergencies after 4 pm and, knowing the nurses at the center, trying to explain the urgency of her situation was sure to expose her to more ridicule.

As she tossed and turned in bed amidst bouts of fitful sleep, she kept warding off the specter of herself and Kal diseased and wasting away.

But beyond the fear of disease and death was the hollow emptiness she felt within; an internal reflection of how desolate of human relationships she had suddenly become. She longed for the respite of sleep as loneliness, like a shroud of darkness, threatened to eclipse her very sanity.

Ordinarily, she would have watched a movie. This was her usual surefire way to achieving the kind of exhaustion that would inevitably result in sleep. But this particular night, the very thought of a movie repulsed her.

SECTION

9

Redemption

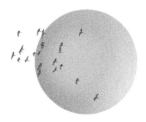

CHAPTER 24

It was 9am when Àshàké left her hostel for the clinic. Her head throbbed from lack of sleep and she was feeling a bit nauseous and dizzy. It was a Saturday and the hospital waiting area was almost deserted. She was not sure a doctor would be available but she spotted a nurse in a scrub suit sorting through a pile of files on a trolley.

The last time she was here she had been brought unconscious from Dr. Mike Kuliji's flat. Now she felt a bit awkward as she approached the Nurse whom she noticed was quite young and pretty.

'Hi, I... ehm want to see a doctor,' she said. 'Oh, I think you're late..." the nurse began to say but was interrupted by a rotund, kind-faced, older nurse coming from a room marked 4. "No, Dr. Ezeani hasn't left yet," she said.

"It's your lucky day, then, dearie," the younger nurse crooned in her sweet sing-song voice, immediately whisking her off to take her vitals.

There was no response when she knocked gently on the door of Consulting Room 4. When she noticed that the door was slightly ajar, she pushed gently and walked in, shutting the door quietly behind her.

Dr. Ezeani didn't look up.

Àshàké stood for about a minute staring down at the glistening waves of his close-cut hair as he sat engrossed in a silver laptop. "Sister, is there a problem?" he asked, still engrossed in his laptop but sensing her presence. "It is not Sister…," Àshàké said, hesitantly. He seemed startled. "Oh, I'm so sorry… I thought it was the nurse," he said rising from his seat.

Staring at her ever so briefly, he had offered her one of the patients' seats across from him. "I'm Kamsy," he said, momentarily extending a hand but, apparently thinking better of it, rubbed his hands together instead. Àshàké, in spite of herself, found his discomfiture and fidgeting a bit amusing.

He was in his mid-twenties, of medium height, and strongly built. There was a finesse about his features that spoke of privilege. It was a characteristic the deprivation of Àshàké's background had conditioned her to immediately recognize. Kamsy Ezeani looked like any one of the rich kids at Johnson. "I just resumed here last week as a Youth Corps doctor," he said needlessly. He was still standing.

"What's with the frequent abortions?" he asked when he finally sat down. It had taken Àshàké a few moments to catch on. Apparently, he already looked at her medical records. "I'm feeling unwell," she said, evading his question.

"I can see that," he said, his eyes searching her face. "I think I need to run a test," she tried again. "What test exactly?" He asked, sounding slightly amused. Àshàké was beginning to think he was smug and judgmental and that exasperated her.

"My fiancée died last week… and I have nowhere…and my boyfriend threw me out last night…" she blurted out. Her voice broke before she could finish and despite her best effort, she could not rein in her emotions. The weight of her present reality seemed to come crashing down on her as she gave vent to her pent-up frustrations and fears in torrents of tears. Kamsy just sat there; waiting.

He listened as she gave a tearful and disjointed account of the series of life events that culminated in her clinic visit. His expression was one of sadness and deep empathy. Taking the distressed young woman in his arms and comforting her would have been the most natural thing to do, yet he refrained - instead handing her paper towels when she needed them.

Months later as they were out on one of their walks discussing their wedding plans, she had, out of curiosity, asked him how he could be so detached. With his signature mischievous grin, he had said, "it is good for a man not to touch a woman… but just wait till I put that ring on your finger." He had taken off before she could punch him.

That first encounter at the clinic changed her on so many levels. Kamsy had reassured her - after she managed to pull herself together - that everything was going to be alright. There was so much compassion and such reassuring confidence about his person.

He stayed constantly in touch all through the two intervening days before she was due to see him again to review her test results. Though he never called, he sent funny stickers and animated GIFs to liven her mood, text messages to ask how the headache was, whether she still cried, and even what she ate.

With a series of about nine well-timed messages, he provided, without being obtrusive, a much-desired company in what would ordinarily have been a harrowing two-day wait. When, on the night before her clinic visit, she finally yielded to the temptation to call him, he didn't take nor return the call. She had smiled wryly to herself as she wondered why she felt a bit hurt.

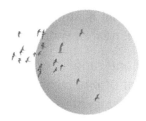

CHAPTER 25

Àshàké didn't attend her morning classes on Monday before keeping her twelve-noon appointment. Despite Kamsy's reassurances, the potential outcome of her screening tests weighed heavily on her mind. Besides, she didn't want to risk running into Kal before knowing her status.

Although it was past mid-day, the reception of the health center was teeming with staff and students and the nurses seemed overwhelmed by the Monday morning rush. She felt quite self-conscious as several familiar, and not-so-familiar students called out their greetings. She noticed someone waving at her from the crowded Nurse's Station down the hall. It was the pretty nurse she had seen two days earlier.

"Dr. Ezeani has your file; he took it this morning," she informed her when she eventually managed to elbow her way through the small crowd to reach her. Àshàké wanted to ask her about her test results but an elderly professor she was attending to was becoming impatient and the students in the badly formed queue were getting restless.

As she stepped to the side to decide what to do next, her phone rang. It was Kamsy. "I saw you come in but it's a very busy clinic this morning," he said. "How are my results?" she asked, trying hard to suppress her anxiety. There was no response. He seemed to have been distracted by someone as Àshàké could hear them conversing. She was getting frantic. "H-h-hello! hello!" her voice had risen and she could sense several pairs of eyes turning in her direction.

"Sorry Àshàké I was seeing a patient," he said when he finally came back on, "I'll meet up with you this evening and explain." The line had promptly gone dead. She wanted to redial his number but steeled herself not to though she was, at that point, near desperate.

It was 2.15pm when her phone rang. "I'm outside," he said. Her heart skipped. *Had she heard a hint of pity in his voice? Why did he choose to bring the results personally?* Kamsy stepped out of his car, a small black SUV when he saw her approaching. He was dressed in jeans, a simple white cotton shirt, and tennis shoes.

Àshàké was seeing him in good light for the first time and, in spite of herself, she thought he was what the girls at Johnson would call a "Clean Guy." She searched his face as she approached; looking for signs of bad news. He seemed to follow her movements with his eyes as she walked the few meters to reach him but his face was inscrutable.

"How are my results?" She asked, her voice slightly shaky. There was an unyielding lump of fear in her throat. "You are good; at least, where that is concerned,' he said.

"Doctor, please let me know... what does that mean?" she pleaded. "How bad is it?" "Your results are good. I'm talking about school... how will you pay your way through now?" he asked.

She didn't wait to hear the last part. With a spontaneity that surprised even her, she hugged him tightly, burying her face in his chest. "Thank you, Doctor... I'm so grateful, thank you..." she kept muttering as she sobbed. "I don't care about graduation... I'm just glad to be alive!"

Kamsy did not attempt to hold her. In retrospect, she imagined he must have been a bit embarrassed just standing there with his hands hanging by his sides while she drenched his shirt with her tears. But he was too kind a soul to stop her or push her away. The awkwardness had suddenly dawned on her. What was she thinking? "Oh, I'm s-so, so sorry, Doctor," she said as she let go, deliberately avoiding looking at his face.

She wondered what he must think of her given all she already told him. "I didn't mean to..." she began again, feeling a need to explain even if she didn't have an explanation. "It's fine," he said, gently cutting in. "I think you'll need this." He was holding out a hankie. When she reached for it, he took her hand instead and squeezed it in that reassuring way she was to become so accustomed to. "I'll see how I can help, we'll talk tomorrow," he said.

Àshàké expected nothing, but the empathy of this kind doctor had become an unexpected anchor in what would have been a season of utter despondency. Overwhelmed by a mixture of different emotions, she could only nod her head as she struggled to stem the flow of her tears.

That evening, she had sent Kal a short text message. *Tests are out and I'm fine.* When after two days she got no response from him, she knew it really was over between them. Although the signs were plain from the outset, she had hoped her clarified health status would have made things right between them. But Kal was done and she was now trash – a fleeting fancy.

She felt hurt.

CHAPTER 26

It seemed Kamsy had swung into action immediately.

"I asked Mom to speak to Dame Maryam Abubakar about placing you on the Chancellor's scholarship for the remaining year," he told her at lunch the next day. She had suspended her macaroni-laden fork on its way to her mouth and gradually set it back on the plate. "Doctor, I don't get…" she said, mouth slightly agape as she tried to make sense of what he was saying.

"First off, can we swap 'doctor' for, say, 'Kamsy'?" he asked, raising his hand to interrupt her. His smiling eyes were gazing right into hers. She slowly nodded and then mouthed the name, "Kamsy." They both laughed. He had gone on to tell her how his mother and the Chancellor's wife go back a long way - first as high school roommates at Queen's Academy and later undergraduates at Premier College of Arts.

"But Mom didn't buy it," he said, "not after I told her your story — a bit of it," he added almost apologetically. Àshàké's eyes were brimming over with tears. Why would this rich doctor she only just met care about a homeless girl with no background? Family friends with Johnson Idris Abubakar? It was unbelievable!

She had spent almost three years at Johnson and she, like most of the other students, had never met the chancellor — beyond the statue at the quadrangle. "I don't know what to say, Doctor...," she began, "Kamsy," he interrupted her, "short for Kamsiyochukwu!" She smiled through her tears. "Okay, Kamsy, I appreciate your concern but I'll be fine."

Though she knew he had a point, just being alive and well after all that happened was all that mattered to her. "You won't be fine, Àshàké." His voice was emphatic. "It will be tight, but we'll find a way around it."

Àshàké was sure he didn't know what he was talking about. With the huge tuition and living expenses at Johnson, she was pretty sure that the unceremonious end of her academic journey at Johnson was in sight and, amazingly, she didn't care. "Kamsy, I see your heart and, trust me, I appreciate this, but you hardly even know me," Kamsy's raised hand stopped her again. "Àshàké, I know enough about you to see why you must get your degree," he said, "out there, it is your only chance."

True to his word and, as she was soon to find out, his character; Kamsy had set in motion an elaborate plan and pursued it with unwavering commitment.

Àshàké's background had conditioned her to live a day at a time and to take life as it came. So, while the well-timed 'anonymous' deposits in her account - which were obviously from Kamsy, though he wouldn't discuss them - helped tide her over to the end of the third year, she had braced herself for the inevitable.

Come the Saturday after exams, all students would be required to vacate the hostels.

Friday night was Vacation Prep Night at Johnson and the hostels were agog as students packed and made vacation get-together plans. The sense of anticipation as everyone looked forward to seeing parents again heightened her own feeling of hopelessness and despondency.

As she absent-mindedly stuffed her suitcases with her clothes, she smiled wryly to herself at the irony of her situation. With her large collection of beautiful clothes, thanks to Hajiya, she could have passed for the wealthier of the largely privileged students at Johnson, yet she didn't have parents or even a home to call her own.

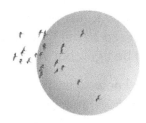

CHAPTER 27

That evening Kamsy called.

He would pick her up at the Founders' Quadrangle by 8am. "Where are we going?" She inquired. "Just be there with your luggage or aren't you going home?" Àshàké could imagine he was laughing and, though she was in no mood for his unending humor, home – wherever that was – sounded good.

The next morning, he was there on the dot of eight and they had driven to a cluster of beautiful detached small bungalows tucked away in a nest of dense foliage at the eastern corner of the campus just by the Vice Chancellor's lodge. A weather-worn wooden sign at the entrance to the driveway said *Council Chalets*.

The shrill chirping of numerous birds as they flew between trees welcomed them and the crunching sound of the dry leaves that covered the driveway announced their approach. There was something about the isolated group of about ten small bungalows, with their mostly leaf-covered lawns and walkways that reminded Àshàké of a scene from a crime thriller.

"Here we are," Kamsy announced as he brought the car to a stop in front of the one marked *Number 5* and started off-loading the trunk.

"Where is this place?" Àshàké asked as she explored the perimeter of the building. "They were originally designed to provide self-catering hospitality for council members but I understand that, though still well maintained, the council members hardly use them; preferring rather to stay at the 5-star Johnson Suites and Towers down the road from the campus gate whenever they had business at the university." Kamsy by now had her full attention.

"When Mom visited me at the doctors' quarters at NAS, she insisted the environment was untidy and that the rooms were poorly ventilated." "So, they gave you this place, instead?" Àshàké asked, incredulously. "Well, yes and no. It *is* Mom's complementary chalet. She serves on the council of Johnsons." He told her.

Àshàké stood in the middle of the well-kept sitting room while Kamsy went back outside to bring in the last suitcase. She tried to take in the simple but elegant furnishing while processing all Kamsy had just told her.

Her mind wandered to Mike Kuliji's flat at NAS and all that had happened there. Although it was just a few months before, she felt like she had been suddenly time-warped to an alternative reality. This was worlds away from Non–Academic Staff Flat 14. But then, Kamsy Ezeani wasn't Mike Kuliji.

"A penny for your thoughts," he said as he stepped out of the guest convenience, wiping his wet hands with a towel. She had momentarily lost all awareness of his presence. "I-I don't know, Kamsy. This is too much and your mom... she may not like me here... with you," her voice was shaky with emotion.

He put his hand on her shoulder and gently turned her around. He was just an inch or two taller than she was. There was a kindness in his eyes that invited her to be vulnerable. Yet his hands, firmly but gently, holding her just above the elbows, kept her tumultuous emotions in check. "Àshàké, this place is all yours. I could only survive here for a week. I got tired of the birds and moved back to civilization," he said, smiling into her worried face.

He had gone on to give her a tour of the house. The two bedrooms each had a king-sized bed and a couch. The drawers had clean sheets, blankets, towels, and even bathrobes. The tour ended in the kitchen. "I took the liberty of getting you an electric cooker," he said as he picked up a slim carton on the small kitchen table and carefully slid out a dual-plate electric cooker. "The fridge is stocked and you'll find other supplies in the kitchen cupboards. Make yourself at home."

The entire experience left Àshàké with a certain sense of *de javu*. She had been here before. Her mind strayed to Faruk and Fatima and a dark pall of depression threatened to envelop her yet again. When Kamsy left soon afterward for the clinic, she sat on the sitting room sofa and thought about how short-lived all of this was most probably going to be.

A well-arranged row of books on the table of the bigger bedroom was all that was left of Kamsy's previous short stay in the house. She had languidly gone through the volumes later in the evening. *Clinical Methods, On Call in the ICU*. The rest were Christian literature and a paperback bible. She had gently pulled the bible from the shelf and absent-mindedly thumbed through it.

Kamsy attended New Testament Fellowship about a mile from the campus. She had met Ken Henshaw, the pastor; a rather unremarkable gentleman with what Àshàké considered exaggerated good manners. He would occasionally come to campus for visitations. She remembered asking Kamsy why he would rather worship there than at the University Chapel. "The word at NTF is richer," he said.

"Excuse me! Our chaplain is a professor of comparative religion!" Àshàké had retorted, genuinely surprised at his reason. Kamsy had smiled patiently.

As she made to replace the bible, a piece of yellow sticky note paper, just inside the front cover caught her eye.

I'm off to the airport, Son. Hugs, Mom.

Àshàké smiled. *Ajebo*, Mummy's boy. She thought to herself.

Although she thought it would be more appropriate to use the other bedroom, she felt an inexplicable pull to this room that Kamsy had used – and the bed he had slept in. There was a comfort, almost an intimacy, she felt as she tidied the room up and snuggled under the covers later that evening.

That night he didn't call but sent a message to check on her. *I wish you were here;* she replied. She got a voice note in reply: *wishes aren't horses* and he had laughed in his booming voice.

Kamsy came after work on Monday with packs of assorted foods, bars of chocolate, and a bowl of ice cream. When he saw her still in pajamas, with hair disheveled, sitting on the floor by the entrance, he knew something was wrong. Shutting the door with his foot, he set the packs on the floor and tried to get her to stand. "Àshàké, are you okay?" He asked, instinctively looking her over.

"I thought you were different!" she screamed, pounding on his chest with her fist as she tried to fight him off. "How could you abandon me here like this?" her body was quivering under the loose-fitting pajamas as she sobbed and sniffled. "I didn't abandon you, Àshàké!" he tried to soothe her, completely nonplussed. "I've been on call at the hospital."

He finally managed to calm her enough to lead her gently into the living room and settle her on the couch. But she held onto him; nesting her face in the side of his neck. With his arms loosely around her, Kamsy could still feel the involuntary heaving of her body as the sobs escaped her.

"Why does everyone leave me? Why do they treat me like this?" She asked, raising her head to search his face through tear-brimmed eyes. Kamsy, overtaken with compassion, could only gently shake his head. This was a deeply scarred young woman, he thought.

He could feel the tears sting his own eyes. Then from deep within, he heard it: *you can't do this, Kamsy.* He knew that voice. Though he felt such protectiveness towards this thinly–clad young woman who had been so battered by life, he was also conscious of his own immediate vulnerability.

"I'm here, Àshàké" he whispered as he tenderly picked off strands of wet hair from her sweaty face, "you'll be fine, I promise." "But Faruk, Silas, Kal they all left..." she murmured, her body still quivering slightly as she buried her face in his neck again. Kamsy had stroked her hair briefly, acutely aware of the suppleness of her full breasts against his chest.

"I won't leave, Àshàké," he said, gently holding her away from him. It had taken all his practiced willpower not to take her back in his arms when he saw the hurt in her eyes. Wishing his voice was steadier, he said, "I'll look after you."

When Àshàké spoke again, she was calm. "I'm sorry, Kamsy. I couldn't help myself." He nodded his understanding, smiling. "Now, you go on and freshen up," he said, "there's plenty to eat."

They spent the rest of the evening together, later driving around the now nearly-deserted 750-acre campus of Johnson after buying some *suya* - the barbecued spiced meat delicacy, at the University Staff Club. Àshàké was amazed at how little she knew the campus after three years.

When he finally walked her up to the door later that evening, she had asked him in. "Kamsy, you can go to work from here tomorrow," she pressed him. "No, I need to go, Àshàké. I have a busy day at work tomorrow and an evening service by six," he explained.

"That means you won't see me tomorrow; yet, you want to leave this early?" she asked with a mock baby pout. "It's 9pm. We've been together since two!" He reminded her, showing her his watch.

"Okay stay till 10pm, pleeeease," she begged, gently tugging at his tie. He capitulated: "One more hour and that's it," he said. "Deal!" she said, as she playfully pulled him by his tie into the house.

That evening marked a turning point in their relationship.

CHAPTER 28

Kamsy hadn't sat down after Àshàké disappeared into the bedroom. He had busied himself trying to get the cable TV to work. "I didn't know you subscribed," she said from behind him. He hadn't heard her come in. "Yes, I did. I thought you might need it," he said, scrolling through the channels to be sure they all worked.

When he turned around, he had immediately covered his face with his hands. "What?" she asked in mock surprise. It had probably been a split second but Kamsy had taken it all in; Àshàké sitting cross-legged on the couch in a short shimmering gray silk nightie; torso thrust slightly forward, one long flawless leg swinging on the other and her bosom firmly outlined against the thin fabric.

"Àshàké... y-you need to go and get dressed," he stuttered, now trying unsuccessfully to keep his focus on her face. She had, instead, stood up and slowly walked towards him.

Kamsy was momentarily transfixed as he watched her walk across the room; hair down around her shoulders, her exquisite body swinging to the rhythm of her steps. "I want you to stay, Kamsy, please stay..." Her voice was husky as her eyes implored him. Kamsy could feel his heart pounding as the sight and sound of her stirred the explosive awakening of long-suppressed appetites. As she reached him, he turned abruptly to the door, "Sorry, Àshàké; I can't do this!" he said and walked out into the night.

Àshàké didn't think she had done anything wrong. She liked Kamsy a lot and had fantasized from the first day about how romantic it would be to share the chalet with him. But she could tell that her little stunt had deeply upset him even if she wasn't sure why.

Kamsy was different. There was a selflessness to his kindness that Àshàké found disconcerting, and a little confusing. The canvas of her own romantic experience was splattered with depressing colors of exploitation and abuse and she hadn't been psychologically prepared for the grace that shone through his untiring benevolence. She felt an instinctive need to surrender even when he made no demands... and to give, even if he never asked.

After four harrowing days of silence, she had resolved to text him an apology on Friday night. When she picked up her phone, she noticed he had sent her an e-receipt, with a short text: *Final year fees sorted. Sorry about Monday night.*

She couldn't hold back her tears. When she finally called, he answered at the first ring. "Hi, Àshàké, sorry I should have called. It's been very hectic at work" he said. "I wanted to thank you for the fees and apologize...," she began, but he had cut in, 'it's not a problem. Can we talk Monday? I'm on call tomorrow and, of course, there's Church the next day.

The three weekly services at NTF were such a big deal for Kamsy. Àshàké, who attended an occasional Sunday service at the University Chapel, had not been able to fathom why everything else, for Kamsy, came second to Church services. "Can I come along to Church on Sunday?" she asked, hesitantly. There was a momentary silence. "Sure," he said finally, "I'll pick you up at 8.30am. Dress nice."

Kamsy was at the house at the dot of 8.30. She had on a purple and red patterned frock with white sneakers. Her hair was bound with an improvised hair band she had made from a twisted red scarf. "What do you think?" she asked, twirling around. "Not bad for a church date," Kamsy said, laughing.

It had taken them under thirty minutes to reach the modified warehouse that housed NTF. Although the service had not started, Àshàké noticed that the auditorium was already filling up with people.

Smartly dressed ushers were moving around making sure everyone was comfortable.

Kamsy handed her over to a dark pretty usher he introduced as Eva and disappeared into an inner room behind the altar. "There's a seat closer to the front," Eva informed her, "or would you rather sit in the middle?" She opted to sit in the middle. Eva helped her download an electronic bible on her phone before giving her a warm hug and going on to receive other people.

Kamsy was the first on the altar. He led a few short prayers and then sang *What a Beautiful Name.* Àshàké was enthralled. That church service was a revelation for her in so many ways: the music, the sermon, the people – she felt like she belonged there. Although Kamsy had a few meetings after the service, Àshàké was never alone. Several people, including Pastor Ken, had walked up to her to say hello and introduce themselves.

About to Wed

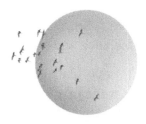

CHAPTER 29

The drive back was mostly in silence.

Although Àshàké would have wanted to spend more time with Kamsy, she felt a strong urge to be alone. "I'm sorry, Kamsy," she said, "I feel terrible about last Monday, I'm so sorry." Kamsy nodded slowly, and then asked, "Did you enjoy the service?" "Yes, but I feel such a void, such a deep yearning. It's difficult to explain."

They had just pulled up at the house. "Give me your hand," he said, and when she did, he said "just repeat after me" and he led her in a short prayer. "I got you this," he said afterward, opening his glove compartment to hand her a beautiful bonded leather bible. "Start from the book of Luke and never stop reading. I'll see you tomorrow."

As she walked to the door, she felt like dancing. There was a song, a sweet, sweet song bubbling up from her inside and, although she didn't know any church songs, she had opened her mouth anyway. What an experience it was as those unfamiliar words burst through and, like cascading streams of refreshing water, drenched the parched grounds of her soul.

When she finally got quiet almost two full hours later, *she knew she was changed.* She could not explain it, yet she knew this was what her heart had always yearned for.

In the months that followed, NTF provided the structure she needed to explore and grow in her new faith. There were Spirit Milk Classes, Neighborhood Cell Meetings, and an array of online discussion groups that addressed everything from sexuality to drugs. Although she had graduated from high school with an A in Christian Religion, the bible seemed to have suddenly come alive and she could hardly get enough.

Àshàké was also helplessly in love with Kamsy and was glad that the second half of his service year at the medical center spanned most of her final year in school. That meant spending a lot of time together; and with that, the intensification of the chemistry between them.

Kamsy was a thinker and the lush greens of the university's serene 18-hole golf course was his favorite place. Àshàké often wondered what he thought about during those long hours he regularly spent there. "I think about the scriptures, the future, and, very often these days, you," he told her as they sat on the soft grass the first day he took her there. "aaawh, how sweet..." she said, pleased.

That was the first time Kamsy was verbalizing any feelings for her although they now saw each other virtually every day and spent a lot of time together. When she moved closer and rested her head on his shoulder, he had put his hand around her waist and turned to stare at her. "I think God created you on the seventh day," he said meditatively as he turned again to stare into the distance. "Is that a good or a bad thing," Àshàké asked, slightly puzzled. "Good," he said, "you are very pretty."

"That sounds sooo... well, unromantic, Dr. Ezeani," Àshàké said, poking at his chest with her fingers. "And, how does 'romantic' sound, Juliet?" he asked, turning to face her on the grass, a mischievous grin on his face. "Like a kiss on the lips on this deserted golf course." She replied, looking up at him. "Be careful what you wish for," he said, rising and pulling her to her feet. "It is time to go."

Àshàké was no longer the girl she was that Monday night in Chalet 5, but she still caught herself occasionally fantasizing about Kamsy. As their relationship grew, they had had several frank discussions about singlehood, sexuality, and premarital celibacy on one hand and God's standards on the other. For a man as attractive and as privileged as he was, Àshàké couldn't help but admire Kamsy's deliberate resolve to live his beliefs.

Yet, he was totally supportive of her even in her occasional missteps; never condescending, never judgmental. With Kamsy, Àshàké felt valued and unconditionally loved.

CHAPTER 30

While NTF, with its multiple targeted ministries to singles and young people, was a veritable support structure as Àshàké worked her way out of her mental morass of sexual entanglements, she still had those unguarded moments when those 'demons' would resurrect and try to mire her again in concupiscent longings now forbidden.

"I can't take this anymore," she told Kamsy on phone one night, "this craving is killing me."

"Just keep growing till you outgrow them," he said, "the mind programming took a while... it also takes a process to uninstall." Àshàké had gotten tired of hearing that. "I wish you'll stop being so patronizing," she quipped. But Kamsy seemed to have just one remedy for every single one of the pressures she faced in those early months. "Change your diet from *world* to *word*," he would say.

He always insisted that, if she would take advantage of all NTF offered, and invest in personal prayers and bible study consistently, she would do well. "The beauty of genuine growth in any area of life, Àshàké, is that it is never dramatic; It just happens," he would say.

True to his word, the transformation had started quite early. Although Àshàké didn't feel different *per se*, the response of people to her was different. There seemed to be a curiosity, almost a confusion - especially within her former circle - about what exactly happened to her.

Kal was the most affected.

He had been glad when he learned she hadn't been diagnosed with anything transmissible and had also suspected - even hoped - she would not be resuming for their final session. Everything in Johnson was expensive, from tuition to living expenses, and Kal was sure she had zero chances of getting that kind of funding from any other source.

But the Àshàké that resumed for final year was a far cry from the broken and traumatized girl that had fled his apartment just three months earlier. Her physical appearance, while still elegant, was noticeably understated, and there was a new radiance; a warmth, that she exuded.

Kal was not quite sure how to relate with her after all that happened. He was therefore surprised, if not a little confused, that their initial interaction was devoid of any kind of tension. She was warm, wanted to be sure he got her messages about the test results, and seemed particularly interested in how he spent the long vacation.

Not one given to unsatisfied curiosity, he had asked her: "Àshàké, what exactly happened to you?" "I survived," she said with a short laugh. "Obviously," Kal insisted, "but I don't mean just that... there's something else... you are different. Or is it the doctor?" Àshàké was really laughing now. "Don't tell me you've been snooping on me!" she said. "Naa! Heard you were hanging out, and then he attended to my ulcers the other day," he said, trying hard to sound dismissive. Cool dude... not my type, though." Àshàké sensed jealousy.

"I met Jesus," she said.

He blinked, staring at her for a few seconds as if she just smacked him across the face. "You met who?" he asked as if to confirm he heard right. "I got born again Kal. I'm a Christian now; that was what happened to me." By now, he was rolling his eyes and shaking his head all at once.

"Babe, get outta here!" he said incredulously, "I know you; you aren't the type for that kind of crap!" He waved her away and went to join his friends at the other end of the lecture hall, still occasionally looking at her and shaking his head.

Àshàké smiled to herself. Kal was superficial and self-centered. It was difficult to imagine that, for six months, she had practically eaten out of his hand; submitting to his every whim and satisfying his every fantasy. But then, as they say, they were birds of the same feather.

But now, what a sweet disruption her life has been through in just three months! And those classes at NTF; what a sense of value and self-worth they have instilled in her! Between Christ and Kamsy, she felt like the best thing the world ever saw.

Although the woman in her desired more from Kamsy, she knew that what he had given already – even if it was all he gave – was more than enough. As that familiar joy bubbled up on her inside and her eyes began to fill with tears - as they often did these days; she began to hum that favorite song of hers,

You brought me out from the miry clay;

You set my feet on a rock to stay;

You put a song in my mouth to sing;

A song of praise,

Halleluiah...

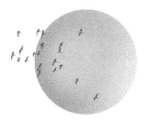

CHAPTER 31

Àshàké was glad to return to the hostel at the beginning of the new school year. "I kept thinking your mom would find me here one day and throw me out," she told Kamsy the day he came to move her luggage. "She knew you were here all along," he replied, "I just felt you'll be more relaxed believing she didn't."

Àshàké deeply resented that. She resented the idea that Kamsy would make her indebted to this rich mother of his who must think very little of her. So, when he informed her a few weeks later that his mother was in the university for council business and would want to have dinner with them, she panicked. But he had squeezed her hand reassuringly, and said, "She asked to meet you."

Dinner was at the restaurant of Johnson Hotels and Suites. Mrs. Ezeani was still up in her suite when they arrived and the manager, who obviously knew Kamsy well, had personally led them to the reserved table. As Àshàké took in the well-appointed restaurant and its exquisite ambience, she wondered what it must have cost to create such extravagant luxury.

When Mrs. Ezeani later walked into the restaurant, she looked around and then waved and smiled when she saw them. She was a tall pretty woman and Àshàké liked how her cream loose-fitting gown flowed to the floor almost completely concealing a pair of white fur slippers.

She stopped at a counter by the entrance; her phone, all the while, supported between her left ear and shoulder as she spoke and scribbled on a tablet with a stylus pen all at once. She would wave and smile at them occasionally while her call lasted.

"Mom! She never rests!" Kamsy said, shaking his head. Àshàké said nothing. She was too preoccupied with her impending encounter with Mrs. Ezeani.

They both stood up when they saw her approaching. "Pardon me, my dears," she said when she finally got to the table. "I had to get that out of the way," she said, as she put away her iPad. "Hello, son, *kedu ka I mere*? How are you?" She asked; giving Kamsy a long tight hug; fondly rubbing his back all the while. "And this must be Àshàké," she said, turning to her and hugging her. Àshàké thought she smelt of a thousand fragrant flowers.

She had briefly held Àshàké away from her and looked her over. "Impeccable features, my dear," she said, "And those hoops of yours, they look perfect," she said, briefly pointing at her earrings, as she took a seat Kamsy had pulled out for her. "Thank you, *Nna*. You know Àshàké reminds me of those days when I used to be trimmer," she said with a short laugh as she invited them to sit.

"You are still one of the most beautiful women I know, Mom," Kamsy said, looking serious. "*Anugo m*, I've heard you," she said playfully, slapping his shoulder. "You and your father should stop deceiving this old woman." They both laughed.

Àshàké wore a polite smile but stayed silent throughout the initial exchange. Although Mrs. Ezeani was surprisingly warm and friendly, she felt a bit intimidated in the presence of this elegant and classy woman whose son had, in three short months, transformed her world with his kindness. For some odd reason, her mind strayed to Hajiya Meiro. *What a contrast*, she thought.

Within a matter of minutes though, she was completely at ease with her.

Àshàké was surprised that she didn't ask any questions about her parents or her background - questions she had strenuously rehearsed for. Rather she spoke fondly of her own school days, meeting her husband, and even giving birth to Kamsy.

Àshàké was amazed at the easy chemistry between mother and son and her vast knowledge of modern trends. She had connected with her on Instagram and added her to a forum she hosted for aspiring young female leaders on Facebook.

Although Mrs. Ezeani ate very little herself, she had made sure that there was more than enough for them to eat.

"I hear my son wants to marry you," she said, seemingly out of the blue. She was dabbing the corners of her mouth with a napkin and there was a mischievous glint in her eyes as she looked at Kamsy. "Mom!" Kamsy screamed, rolling his eyes in utter disbelief.

"I don't know...," Àshàké stuttered, completely nonplussed as Mrs. Ezeani gently took her hand. "Shhhhhh," she hushed her, "let's not ruin it. He'll still ask you. Isn't that right, *Nna*?" she said, smiling at a now mute Kamsy.

The meeting with Mrs. Ezeani was brief and quite memorable. Because she had meetings to attend the same evening, she had discharged them with some big hugs less than an hour later. But her open acceptance and warmth did wonders for Àshàké's much-battered self-confidence. She had treated her like an equal; a sister.

Both of them were lost in their own thoughts as they drove back to campus. Àshàké didn't think what happened at the restaurant was just part of loose, good-natured banter. Mrs. Ezeani had put a face to what she already knew about her, felt satisfied, and; being the woman she is, had seized the initiative from her son.

She had smiled inwardly at her own self-flattery. The classy Mrs. Ezeani wants her son to marry her! *What are you feeling like?* She chided herself.

Kamsy didn't usually respond to most of his calls and messages, but he always looked at them. "Someone might be in distress," he once told her. So, when his phone screen lit up just as they reached the front of her hostel, he picked it up. "Mom," he said, smiling as he put the phone face-down again.

"What did she say," Àshàké asked, curious. She had imagined she wanted to be sure they were back on campus. In response, Kamsy picked up the phone and handed it to her.

I'm not going to bed until I know she said, yes! The text said.

Àshàké slowly looked at him trying to process the message. "So, is it 'yes,' Àshàké?" he asked, turning to her, as he brought out a tiny glass box seemingly out of nowhere. "I want to love you and protect you for the rest of my life... if you'll do me the honor."

The events of the night had moved a bit too fast for Àshàké and she was feeling slightly emotionally disoriented. Nodding, she said tearfully, "Yes... Kamsy, yes!"

When he slowly slipped the single-studded ring on her middle finger, she felt a deluge of conflicting emotions, and, for the first time, he had taken her in his arms and squeezed her tightly. "I love you Àshàké, I love you very much," he said. That night, not just Mrs. Ezeani, but both of them went to bed with a smile on their faces.

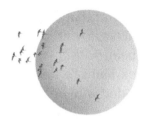

CHAPTER 32

Everything worked smoothly over the following months. Àshàké tidied up at school while Kamsy transited to a surgical residency in Port Harcourt. Àshàké had wished they be wed in NTF but Kamsy had gently declined. "The Ezeanis are a whole community. It will be too much pressure for Pastor and NTF and, besides, I'm sure you'll love my home church," he had assured her.

As the wedding drew closer, they met several family members mostly on Kamsy's side and the experience, for the most part, was pleasant. The preparatory process with Sanctification Chapel was however altogether a different story.

The pre-marital counseling sessions with the duo of Deacon Ojo and Mrs. Chikere were particularly emotionally exhausting. Their scrutiny of her past, in particular, was deep and loveless.

Something about their demeanor as they arrived for the first session had immediately made Àshàké regret the outfit she chose for the meeting.

She had checked with Kamsy and he had told her she looked awesome. His compliments, as always, had made her feel light-headed. But now under the stern scrutiny of their disapproving eyes, she felt partially unclad. Her dark scuba skirt suddenly felt too tight; her silk blouse too sheer.

Involuntarily her left fingers fiddled with the loose top button of her blouse where the pendant of her tiny gold chain accentuated a subtle cleavage. And so began four grueling Saturdays of probing questions.

After the awkward pleasantries of that first day, they had barely settled into their seats when Mrs. Chikere, a retired nurse, fired the first question: "How many men have you been with?" Àshàké had already heard that it was Mrs. Chikere that took Kamsy's delivery at City Clinic, a private medical practice she had founded with her late husband over thirty years earlier. He had warned her of how fiercely protective she always was of him but Àshàké was unprepared for her undisguised hostility.

"I... I... em... don't remember, Madam," she stuttered. "You don't remember, or you can't count?" Deacon Ojo had countered, his pursed lips and his central stub of graying mustache twitching as he peered at her from above the metal rims of his round glasses. "Maybe...em... one, Sir," she momentarily blurted out, her eyes dropping in embarrassment and guilt. She had lied. Yet, despite her obvious discomfiture, they were unrelenting.

They had made her remember and disclose areas of her past she had forgotten and speak of incidents and affairs she had been too ashamed to mention - even to Kamsy. She had feared on occasions that the wedding plans would screech to a halt at that table.

Yet, through it all, Kamsy had remained calm and reassuring. He would constantly squeeze her clammy hands beneath the table in that reassuring manner of his that said, *"It doesn't matter, I'm here now."*

The rest of the sessions weren't any easier. They had badgered her with the most uncomfortable questions as if to prove what a terrible choice Kamsy had made. But He had remained calm and extremely gracious – to them and, even more so, to her.

EPILOGUE

Kamsy's choice of *Chalet 5* of Johnson Council Flats for their honeymoon had come as a surprise to his mother who had more exotic plans. "When the ministers are done with their formalities," he had told her on their wedding eve, "I want to go back and take you up on that tempting offer you made me in the grey nightie that Monday night."

"Backslider!" she had screamed at him, and they had both burst out laughing.

When he finally came out of the bathroom dripping wet and singing Timi Dakolo's *Iyawo Mi,* Àshàké convulsed with laughter as she watched him waltzing around in his birthday suit. "Where were we?" he asked, picking up the edge of the duvet with a flourish. "Your body is dripping-wet, Kamsy, you'll ruin the sheets," she protested, trying unsuccessfully to pull the duvet away from him.

But he burrowed under the sheets and took her in his wet embrace, muffling her giggles as their lips connected.

THE END

Printed in Great Britain
by Amazon

33276326R00071